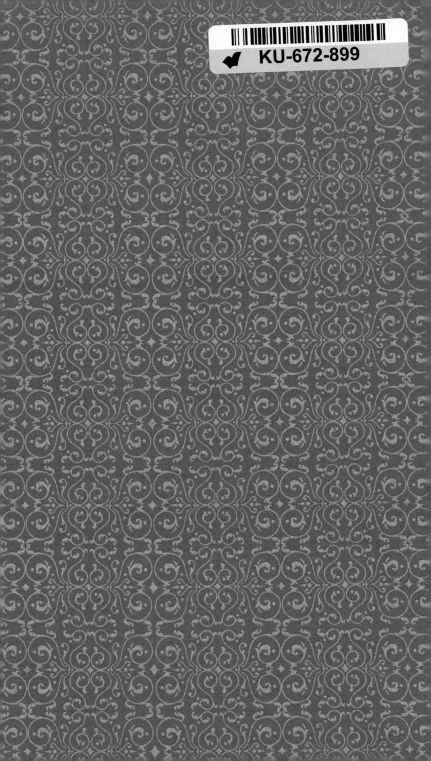

A Collection distributed by Heron Books

THE
GREATEST MASTERPIECES
OF
RUSSIAN LITERATURE

IVAN S. TURGENEV

SMOKE

Translated from the Russian by
Natalie Duddington
with an Introduction by Nikolay Andreyev

Original Illustrations by Marek Rudnicki

Distributed by
HERON BOOKS

Published by arrangement with
J.M. Dent & Sons Ltd.

© *Illustrations, Edito-Service S.A., Geneva*

marek Rudnicki

INTRODUCTION

Smoke was published in the March issue of the journal *The Russian Messenger* in 1867. Turgenev, however, had hit on the idea as early as 1862 when he compiled a preliminary list of the main personages. In his letters over the next few years he frequently mentions the slowness of his work on the novel. The final draft of his manuscript bears the note '*Smoke* was started in November 1865 and finished at the end of January 1867'.

Smoke has always—rightly—been considered both by Russian and European critics to be a *roman à thèse* or even a political pamphlet. The novel is full of scenes which show up often in a very ironical and sarcastic light the various strata of Russian society. At the same time, *Smoke* provides a political commentary on the problems of the day in Russia after the emancipation of the serfs in 1861, and an exposition of the trends of thought of the various groups in educated Russian society.

Turgenev, writing to the radical critic Pisarev in 1867, stresses that he paints his picture of Russia from the heights of European civilization. Potugin (who in *Smoke* more or less expresses the author's own theories) 'will die a dyed-in-the-wool Westernizer, and my works will have been written in vain if a smouldering and unquenchable fire is not felt in him'.

It is not surprising that this criticism of Russian reality on the part of such a liberal-minded admirer of Western culture as Turgenev provoked many attacks on the author of *Smoke*. In a letter to his friend Herzen, (a Russian radical living in self-imposed exile in London), Turgenev wrote in May 1867 that nobody had ever been so unanimously criticized as he had been for *Smoke*: 'Everybody curses me, the reds and the whites and from above and below and from the flanks —particularly from the flanks'. His literary contemporaries and rivals, Tolstoy, Dostoyevsky, Goncharov and the poet Tyutchev all criticized *Smoke* for various reasons, some for its politics and others for its technical deficiencies, and others yet again for the moral lapses and lack of patriotism in the novel. Feelings in Russian society ran so high that certain members of the fashionable English Club in St Petersburg wanted to exclude Turgenev from membership as a protest against *Smoke*.

The novel's significance as a critical evaluation of Russia after the reforms of the 1860's is still valid today, but its more interesting literary worth should perhaps be sought in other aspects of the book. As was usual for Turgenev, the subject of *Smoke* was taken straight from life. Gubaryev, 'a Slavophile, a socialist, a democrat, and anything else you like', represented Ogaryev (a radical whom Turgenev disliked) and Tatyana Shestova is in fact Olga Turgeneva—a distant cousin of the author's whom he very nearly married. As for General Ratmirov and his wife Irina, Turgenev is thought to have been depicting a well-known St Petersburg society beauty, an ex-mistress of the

Emperor Alexander II. Turgenev's publisher was worried by the very obvious portrayal of the Ratmirovs and (according to Turgenev in a letter to Pauline Viardot in April 1867) demanded a series of changes. Turgenev consented to a few minor changes, but reverted for the most part to the original in the later editions of the novel.

Turgenev had at one time thought to call his novel *Two Lives*, for he had become more and more preoccupied with the problem of the relationship between Irina and Litvinov, but the lyrical side of the book, 'two lives united for ever would have sped away into the unknown', gave way to the socio-political element, 'everything suddenly turned into smoke', and the editor of *The Russian Messenger* decided that *Smoke* was a more appropriate title in view of the political interests of the journal's readers.

Nevertheless the 'unquestionably lovely lyricism of *Smoke*', to quote the poet Nekrasov, gives meaning and charm to the whole book. As in his other novels, and particularly in *Fathers and Children* (cf. the Introduction to E.M.L. 742, 1962), Turgenev affirms the strength of love and the tyranny of passion. An interesting new feature of Turgenev's writing occurs in *Smoke*, viz. the negative and positive heroines. Irina departs from the lines of his previous heroines; she does not, as her predecessors usually did, lead the hero to overcome the difficulties in his path—she is merely the embodiment of passion. It is Tatyana who finds happiness through self-sacrifice, and is able to help Litvinov to find a measure of his self-respect.

The effect of love is stronger than anything else in

Smoke, and is in fact the only reality in the novel, for when love fails everything turns into 'smoke': all the theories, the relationships, even Russia itself.

NIKOLAY ANDREYEV.

Cambridge, 1964.

SMOKE

THE NAMES OF THE CHARACTERS IN THE BOOK

Grigóry Miháilovitch (or Miháilitch) Litvínov
Irína Pávlovna Osínin
Victórinka
Cleopátrinka
Tatyána Petróvna (Tánya) Shestóv
Kapitolína Márkovna
Rostisláv Bambáev
Semyón Yákovlevitch Voroshílov
Stepán Nikoláevitch Gubaryóv
Dorimedónt Nikoláevitch Gubaryóv
Matryóna Semyónovna Suhánchikov
Tit Bindásov
Pishchálkin
Sozónt Ivánovitch (or Ivánitch) Potúgin
Valerián Vladímirovitch Ratmírov

I

On 10th August 1862, at four o'clock in the afternoon a number of people were crowding in front of
the famous *Conversation* at Baden-Baden.   The weather
was lovely; everything around—the green trees, the
light-coloured houses of the cosy town, the undulating
hills—lay spread out in festive abundance in the rays
of the gracious sunshine; everything smiled with a
kind of blind and trustful charm, and the same vague
but kind smile hovered on human faces, old and
young, ugly and handsome.   Even the painted and
powdered Parisian *cocottes* did not disturb the general
impression of rejoicing and serene content, and the
many-coloured ribbons, feathers, gold, and tinsel, on
hats and veils, suggested to the eye the lively brilliance
of lightly swaying spring flowers and rainbow-
coloured wings.   Only the dry guttural crackle of
French conversation heard an all sides could neither
replace the twittering of birds nor be compared with it.

Everything, however, went on in its usual way.
The orchestra in the pavilion played selections from
La Traviata, a waltz of Strauss, and then *Tell her*, a
Russian song, instrumented by an obliging conductor.
In the gambling halls the same familiar figures crowded
round the green-baized tables with the same dull and
greedy look of something between amazement and
exasperation—an essentially predatory look which the

gambling fever imparts to all, even the most aristocratic, features. The same stoutish and smartly
dressed Russian landowner from Tambov, with the
same incomprehensible, convulsive haste, leaned over
the table, staring blankly in front of him, and, taking
no notice of the cold smiles of the croupiers, scattered
with a perspiring hand gold coins in all the four
corners of the roulette at the very moment when '*Rien
ne va plus!*' was declared, thus depriving himself of
any chance of winning even in case of luck. This did
not in the least prevent him that very evening from
supporting with sympathetic indignation Prince Kokó,
one of the well-known leaders of the aristocratic
opposition—the Prince Kokó who in Paris, in
Princess Mathilde's salon, in the presence of the
emperor, remarked so happily: '*Madame, le principe
de la propriété est profondément ébranlé en Russie.*'

In their usual way our amiable compatriots gathered
round the Russian tree—*l'arbre russe*; they approached
it haughtily and negligently, in fashionable style; they
greeted one another majestically, with elegant ease,
as befits beings who are at the very summit of modern
culture. But once they had met and sat down, they
had absolutely nothing to say to one another and fell
back either upon pitiful tittle-tattle or the hackneyed,
flat, and extremely impudent jokes of a hopelessly
stale French ex-journalist, a babbler and buffoon, with
wretched Jewish shoes on his puny little feet and a
contemptible little beard on his ignoble little face. He
served up *à ces princes russes* all kinds of insipid rubbish
out of the old almanacs *Charivari* and *Tintamarre*, and
the *princes russes* went off into peals of grateful laughter

2

as though involuntarily recognizing the overwhelming superiority of foreign wit and their own utter incapacity to invent anything amusing. And yet they numbered among them all the *fine fleur* of our society, all 'the best and most fashionable people.' Among them was Count X, our incomparable dilettante, a deep and musical nature, who 'recited' songs so divinely, though in truth he could not play two notes correctly without first prodding the piano keys at random with his forefinger, and sang like an inferior gipsy or a Parisian hairdresser. There was also our delightful Baron Z, a Jack of all trades—writer, administrator, orator, and card-sharper. There was Prince Y, a friend of the people and of the Church, who in the happy old days of state monopolies amassed an enormous fortune by selling vodka mixed with dope; and the brilliant general O. O., who had conquered somebody, restored order somewhere, but now did not know what to do with himself or what to say for himself; and R. R., an amusing stout man who imagined himself to be very ill and very intelligent, while in truth he was strong as an ox and dull as a post. This R. R. was almost the only man of his day to have kept the traditions of the 'society lions' of the forties, of the period of *A Hero of our Times* and Countess Vorotynsky: he preserved the gait with the swing on the heels, *le culte de la pose* (it cannot even be said in Russian), an unnaturally slow way of moving, a majestically sleepy expression on his immobile, as it were offended-looking, face, the habit of interrupting other people with a yawn, of scrutinizing his own finger-nails, of suddenly giving a nasal laugh and shifting his hat from the back of his head on to his eyebrows, and so on, and so on.

There were important government officials among them, diplomats, great personages of European fame, men of wisdom and council who imagined that the Golden Bull was issued by the Pope and that the English 'poor rate' was levied on the poor. There were, too, some zealous but shy admirers of the *dames aux camélias*, young society lions dressed in the real London fashion, with fine partings down the back of their heads and splendid long whiskers—young lions whom one would have thought there was nothing to prevent being as vulgar as the notorious French babbler; but no! we evidently do not care for home-products, and Countess S, the famous lawgiver of fashion and *grand genre*, nicknamed maliciously 'Queen of the Wasps' and 'Medusa in a bonnet,' preferred, in the absence of the French wit, to address herself to the numerous Italians, Moldavians, American spiritualists, sprightly secretaries of foreign embassies, young Germans with effeminate but prematurely cautious faces, and so on. The example of the countess was followed by Princess Babette, the one in whose arms Chopin breathed his last (there are reckoned to be about a thousand ladies in Europe in whose arms he expired), and by Princess Annette, who had everything in her favour except that at times, like the smell of cabbage overpowering the finest perfume, a plain washerwoman suddenly came to the surface in her; and Princess Pachette, who had had such a misfortune: her husband was given a prominent post, and all of a sudden, *Dieu sait pourquoi,* he thrashed the mayor of

4

the town and stole 20,000 roubles of Government money; and the young Princess Zizi prone to laughter, and the young Princess Zozo prone to tears; they all turned a cold shoulder to their compatriots and left them alone. . . . Let us too leave those charming ladies alone and move further off from the famous tree round which they sit in such expensive though somewhat tasteless attire, and may the Lord grant them relief from the boredom that consumes them!

II

A few steps away from the Russian tree, a good-looking man of about thirty, lean and dark, of medium height, with a manly and pleasant face, was sitting at a small table by the Café Weber. Bending forward and resting both hands on his cane he sat simply and calmly like a man to whom it does not even occur that any one might notice him or concern himself with him. He slowly gazed about him, slightly screwing up his large, expressive hazel eyes in the sunshine, or steadily following some eccentric passer-by, while a quick, almost childish smile faintly stirred his small moustache and lips and his prominent short chin. He was wearing a loose coat of German make; a soft grey hat half concealed his high forehead. At the first glance he produced the impression of an honest, efficient, and rather self-confident young man such as there are a good many in the world. He appeared to be resting after a long spell of work, and was enjoying the scene before him all the more simple-heartedly because his thoughts were far away and moved in a world that was very different from his present surroundings. He was Russian; his name was Grigory Mihailovitch Litvinov.

We have to be introduced to him and so must give a short account of his very simple and uneventful past.

He was the son of a retired civil servant, of humble

extraction, but was brought up in the country, and not in town as might be expected. His mother belonged to the nobility and was educated at a government school for daughters of gentlemen; she was extremely kind and sentimental, but she certainly had character. Twenty years younger than her husband, she re-educated him to the best of her ability, accustomed him to a landowner's, instead of a petty official's, style of living, subdued and softened his harsh and acrid temper. Thanks to her he began to dress neatly, acquired decent manners, and gave up swearing; he came to respect scholars and learning, though of course he never held a book in his hands, and endeavoured in every way not to demean himself; he actually learned to walk more slowly, and to speak in a languid voice, chiefly about exalted subjects—which cost him a great deal of trouble. 'I'd like to give that fellow a thrashing,' he sometimes thought to himself, but he said aloud: 'Yes, yes, of course—it's a problem.'

Litvinov's mother ran her house too in European fashion: she was polite to the servants and did not allow any one to gorge himself to stupefaction at dinner. But neither she nor her husband could do anything with the estate that belonged to her: it had been neglected for years. It was a large estate with meadows, woods, and a lake, which once had a big factory built on it by a zealous but thoroughly impractical owner. It had flourished in the hands of a scoundrelly tradesman and finally perished under the management of a conscientious German who rented it. Madame Litvinov was thankful that at any rate she had not brought her property into a worse state, or run into debt. Unfortunately she had poor health and died of consumption the very year that her son entered the Moscow University.

He did not finish his course there (through circumstances of which the reader will learn later) and returned to the country, where he loitered about for a time without any work, any connections, and almost without friends. In 1855 he was drafted into the militia, thanks to the landowners of his district who were not well disposed to him; they were influenced, not so much by the foreign theory of the evils of absenteeism, as by the home-bred conviction that each should take care of number one. He very nearly died of typhus in the Crimea, where he spent six months in a dug-out on the shores of the Azov Sea, not having seen a single 'ally.' Afterwards he served on the committees of nobility in his district—not without unpleasantness, of course, and, while living in the country, developed a passion for farming. He understood that his mother's estate, badly and indolently managed by his feeble old father, did not yield one-tenth of what it might yield, and that in skilful and experienced hands it would be a regular gold-mine. But he also understood that experience and knowledge were the very things he lacked—and so he went abroad to learn agriculture and technology, learn them from the very beginning. He spent over four years in Mecklenburg, in Silesia, at Carlsruhe, went to Belgium and to England; he worked conscientiously and acquired knowledge. He did not come by it easily, but he had stood the trial to the end, and now,

confident of himself, of his future, of the good he would do to his neighbours, and perhaps even to the whole countryside, he was about to return home. His father, utterly bewildered by the emancipation, by the redivision of lands, by the redemption of property—in short, by the new regime, begged and implored him in every letter to make haste and come back. . . . But why was he at Baden?

He was at Baden because he was expecting from day to day the arrival of his distant cousin and betrothed —Tatyana Petrovna Shestov. He had known her almost from a child and had spent the spring and the summer with her at Dresden where she was living with her aunt. He sincerely loved, he deeply respected his young kinswoman, and after finishing his obscure preparatory work, ready to enter a new field of activity, take up real and not 'official' duties, he offered to her —as to the woman he loved, his friend and his comrade —to unite her life with his, for joy and for sorrow, for rest and for toil, 'for better, for worse' as the English say. She consented, and he went to Carlsruhe where he had papers, books, and luggage to collect. . . . But why was he in Baden, you will ask again?

He was in Baden because Tatyana's aunt who had brought her up, Kapitolina Markovna Shestov—an eccentric maiden lady of fifty-five, the kindest and most genuine of people, a free spirit glowing with the fire of self-sacrifice and abnegation, an *esprit fort* (she read Strauss, though secretly from her niece) and a democrat, a sworn enemy of the smart set and the aristocracy—could not resist the temptation of having just one peep at that smart set in so fashionable a

9

place as Baden. . . . Kapitolina Markovna wore no crinoline and her white hair was cropped like a Russian peasant's, but luxury and brilliance secretly stirred her, and it gave her a thrill of pleasure to despise and abuse them. . . . How could one have refused the treat to the good old lady?

And so that was why Litvinov was so serene and simple, why he looked about him so confidently—his future lay clearly mapped out before him, his life had been definitely planned, and he was proud of this future and rejoiced in it as the work of his own hands.

III

'WELL, well, well! So that's where he is!' he suddenly heard a squeaky voice say almost into his ear, and a plump hand patted him on the shoulder. He raised his head and saw one of his few Moscow acquaintances, a certain Bambaev, a good-natured man of the empty-headed variety, no longer young, with spongy-looking cheeks and nose, dishevelled greasy hair, and a fat flabby body. Always penniless, and always in ecstasies about something, Rostislav Bambaev wandered shouting, but without a purpose, over the face of our long-suffering Mother Earth.

'To think of meeting you here!' he said opening wide his small eyes half hidden by puffy eyelids, and thrusting forward his fat lips over which a dyed moustache stuck out incongruously. 'Well done, Baden! People run to this place like blackbeetles. How did you come here?'

Bambaev was on familiar terms with every one he knew.

'I came here three days ago.'

'Where from?'

'Why do you want to know?'

'Why indeed! But wait a minute, perhaps you don't know who else has come here? Gubaryov! Yes, Gubaryov in person! Just think! He came yesterday from Heidelberg. You know him, of course?'

'I've heard of him.'

'Is that all?   My dear fellow!   We must take you to him at once, this very minute.   Fancy not knowing a man like that!   And here is Voroshilov. . . . Maybe you don't know him either?   I have the honour to introduce you to one another.   You are both scholars! And he is a regular phoenix.   Kiss each other.'

With these words Bambaev turned to a handsome young man standing next to him, with a fresh, rosy, but serious-looking face.   Litvinov stood up and exchanged, not of course a kiss, but a short bow with the 'phoenix' who, to judge by his stern manner, was not too well pleased at this sudden introduction.

'I said "phoenix" and I don't take back my words,' Bambaev went on.   'If you go to Petersburg to the N—— Cadet Corps and look at the list of distinctions whose name will you find at the top?   Semyon   Yakovlevitch   Voroshilov's!   But Gubaryov, Gubaryov, my dear boys, that's the man to whom we must run!   I simply reverence that man!   And not I alone, indeed, but every one.   What a book he is writing now . . . ho-ho-ho!'

'What is it about?' Litvinov asked.

'About everything, my dear man, something like Buckle, you know . . . only deeper and more thorough. . . .   Everything will be settled and made clear in it.'

'But have you read it?'

'No, I haven't, and indeed it's a secret and one shouldn't talk of it; but anything may be expected of Gubaryov, anything!   Yes!' Bambaev sighed and folded his hands.   'If another two or three such intellects were to be found in Russia, my goodness, what wonders might happen! I'll tell you one thing, Grigory Mihailovitch: whatever you may have been doing lately—and I have no idea what you are doing at all—whatever your convictions may be—and I don't know them either—you will find that Gubaryov has something to teach you. Unfortunately he is not staying here long, so we must profit by the opportunity and go to him! Go to him!'

A young dandy with reddish curls and a blue ribbon on his low hat turned round as he passed and looked at Bambaev through his monocle with a mocking smile. Litvinov was annoyed.

'What are you shouting for?' he said. 'You might be hallooing to hounds! I haven't had dinner yet.'

'What of it? We can have it now at Weber's . . . the three of us . . . that'll be fine! Can you pay for me?' he added in an undertone.

'Yes, that's all right, but I really don't know——'

'Oh, nonsense! You'll thank me and he will be pleased, too. Dear me!' Bambaev interrupted himself, 'they are playing the *finale* from *Ernani*. What a lovely thing! . . . *A som . . . mo Carlo!* But what a creature I am! The least thing reduces me to tears. Well, Semyon Yakovlevitch? Voroshilov? Aren't you coming?'

Voroshilov, who was still standing in a pose of graceful immobility, preserving his former proud dignity of mien, significantly lowered his eyes, frowned, muttered something through his teeth . . . but did not say no. Litvinov thought: 'Oh, I may as well do it—my time is my own.'

Bambaev took his arm, but before going to the

café beckoned to Isabella, the famous flower-seller of the Jockey Club: he thought of buying a bouquet from her. But the aristocratic flower-seller did not budge: why should she go up to a man in a soiled velveteen jacket, a spotted cravat, and shabby shoes, who had no gloves on, and whom she had never seen in Paris? Then Voroshilov beckoned to her in his turn; she did go up to him; picking out a tiny bunch of violets from her basket, he tossed a gulden to her. He thought she would be impressed at his lavishness, but she did not stir an eyelid, and as he turned away she pursed up contemptuously her tightly closed lips. Voroshilov was dressed very smartly and even elaborately, but the Parisian's experienced eye immediately detected the absence of real pure-bred chic in his get-up, in his bearing, and in his very walk, which bore traces of early military training.

Settling down in the main hall at Weber's they ordered dinner and entered into conversation. Bambaev talked loudly and enthusiastically of Gubaryov's exalted significance, but soon subsided, and, chewing and sighing noisily, emptied glass after glass. Voroshilov ate and drank little and, as it were, reluctantly, and after questioning Litvinov about his work began to expound his own opinions ... not so much with regard to that work as to various problems in general. He suddenly grew animated and raced along like a spirited charger, emphasizing sharply and with zest every syllable, every letter, like a bright cadet at his final examination, and gesticulating vehemently but inappropriately. Meeting with no interruption he grew more loquacious and lively

14

every minute: he might be delivering a lecture or reading a dissertation. Names of modern scholars, dates of their births and deaths, titles of recently published pamphlets, in short, names, names, names simply poured off his tongue, affording him the greatest delight, reflected in his glowing eyes. Voroshilov obviously despised everything old and valued only the cream of learning, only the last and most advanced achievements of science; it was a real treat to him to mention, however inappropriately, the book by some Dr. Sauerbengel about prisons in Pennsylvania or the article on the Vedas and Puranas in the last issue of the *Asiatic Journal* (he pronounced it in the English way, though of course he knew no English). Litvinov listened and listened, and simply could not make out what was his speciality. One moment he talked of the part played by the Celtic race in history, the next he plunged into the world of antiquity, discussed the Aeginetan marbles, and made much of a predecessor of Phidias, Onatas, who somehow changed into Jonathan, imparting a Biblical or an American flavour to his whole argument; then he suddenly jumped to political economy, calling Bastiat a fool and a rustic, 'no better than Adam Smith and all the physiocrats.'

'Physiocrats?' Bambaev murmured. 'Aristocrats?'

Voroshilov made Bambaev look surprised by casually remarking that Macaulay was antiquated and left far behind by modern historical science; as to Gneist and Riehl, he said it was sufficient to mention them, and he shrugged his shoulders. Bambaev also shrugged his shoulders.

'And all this quite suddenly, apropos of nothing,

15

in a café, before strangers,' thought Litvinov, looking at his new acquaintance's fair hair, light eyes, and white teeth (those large, sugar-white teeth and the clumsily gesticulating hands bothered him most). 'And he hasn't smiled once! But all the same he must be a good lad and quite a greenhorn.'

Voroshilov subsided at last; his youthful voice, high-pitched and hoarse like a young cock's, broke slightly . . . besides, Bambaev began reciting poetry and again very nearly wept, which greatly scandalized an English family sitting at the next table and caused giggles at another, where two *cocottes* were dining with a gentleman who looked like an elderly baby in a lilac wig. The waiter brought the bill; the friends paid.

' Well,' Bambaev exclaimed, getting up heavily from his chair, ' now a cup of coffee and let's be off! But there she is, our Russia,' he added, stopping at the door and pointing enthusiastically with his flabby red hand at Voroshilov and Litvinov. ' Fine, isn't she?'

' Yes, Russia,' Litvinov thought, and Voroshilov, who had again assumed a preoccupied expression, gave a condescending smile and slightly clicked his heels.

Five minutes later the three of them were mounting the stairs of the hotel where Stepan Nicolaevitch Gubaryov was staying. A tall, graceful lady in a hat with a short black veil was walking quickly down the same stairs. Seeing Litvinov she suddenly turned round to him and stopped as though struck with amazement. Her face flushed for a moment and then grew pale as rapidly under the close mesh of the lace. But Litvinov did not notice her, and the lady hastened her pace as she ran down the wide steps.

16

IV

'I COMMEND to you Grigory Litvinov, a regular Russian with no guile in him,' exclaimed Bambaev, introducing Litvinov to a short, thickset man standing in the middle of an excellently furnished room. He looked like a country landowner, and was wearing slippers, a short jacket, grey morning trousers, and a shirt unbuttoned at the neck. 'And this,' he added, turning to Litvinov, 'this is he, the one I told you about, you understand? Well, in short, it's Gubaryov.'

Litvinov stared with interest at the great man. At first sight he could not see anything remarkable about him. He saw a respectable and rather stolid-looking gentleman, with a protruding forehead, thick lips, a bushy beard, a broad neck, and prominent eyes with a slanting, downcast look in them. The gentleman grinned, said 'M-m-m . . . yes . . . that's good . . . I'm pleased,' raised his hand to his own face and, turning his back on Litvinov, took a few steps along the carpeted floor, waddling in a curiously slow and stealthy kind of way. Gubaryov had the habit of walking up and down the room, constantly tugging at his beard and scratching it with his long, hard nails.

With Gubaryov there was a lady of about fifty in a shabby silk dress, with an extremely mobile, lemon-yellow face, black hairs on her upper lip, and sharp

17

little eyes ready to pop out of her head; also a solidly
built man sat huddled up in a corner.

'Well, my good Matryona Semyonovna,' began
Gubaryov, turning to the lady; he evidently did not
think it necessary to introduce Litvinov to her.
'What was it you were telling us?'

The lady was called Matryona Semyonovna Suhanchikov; she was a childless widow of humble means
and for the last two years had been travelling from
one country to another. She at once began speaking
with a peculiar, exasperated eagerness.

'Well, so he came to the prince and said to him:
"Your excellency, your rank and position make it
perfectly easy for you to lighten my lot. You cannot
fail to respect the purity of my convictions, and,
anyway, in our day it's simply out of the question
that a man should be persecuted for his convictions!"
he said. And what do you suppose the prince did—
that enlightened, aristocratic dignitary?'

'Well, what did he do?' asked Gubaryov, thoughtfully lighting a cigarette.

The lady drew herself up, and stretched out her
bony right hand with a pointing forefinger.

'He called his footman and said to him: "Take off
this man's coat and keep it for yourself. I make you
a present of it."'

'And the footman took it off?' asked Bambaev
clasping his hands.

'He took it off and kept it. And that was done by
Prince Barnaulov, a wealthy man, an aristocrat, an
official with special powers, a representative of the
government! What are we to expect after that?'

Madame Suhanchikov's feeble little body shook with indignation, her face worked, her wasted bosom heaved spasmodically under the flat corset; her eyes, needless to say, simply danced—but then they did that whatever she might be talking about.

'A crying shame!' Bambaev exclaimed. 'No punishment bad enough for it!'

'M-m-m. . . . It's all rotten from top to bottom,' remarked Gubaryov, without raising his voice, however. 'It isn't exactly punishment . . . other measures . . . are needed.'

'But come, did it really happen?' Litvinov remarked.

'Really happen?' Madame Suhanchikov caught him up. 'But there can't be the slightest doubt of it, not the sli-ightest . . .' she almost doubled herself up to give more emphasis to her words. 'It was told me by a most reliable man—Kapiton Yelistratov, you know him, Stepan Nicolaevitch. He had heard it himself from eye-witnesses of the hideous scene!'

'Which Yelistratov?' Gubaryov asked. 'The one who was at Kazan?'

'Yes, that's the one. I know, Stepan Nicolaevitch, it was rumoured that he took bribes from some contractors or distillers. But then who spread the rumour? Pelikanov! And how can one believe Pelikanov when every one knows that he is simply a spy!'

'No, allow me, Matryona Semyonovna,' Bambaev intervened. 'I am a friend of Pelikanov's, he is no spy.'

'Yes, yes, that's just what he is, a spy!'

'But goodness me, what next!'

'A spy, a spy!' the lady shouted.

' No, no, he isn't! Wait a second, I'll tell you what . . . ' Bambaev shouted in his turn.

' A spy, a spy!' Madame Suhanchikov repeated.

' No, no! Now Tenteleyev—that's different!' Bambaev roared with all his might.

Madame Suhanchikov subsided instantly.

' About that gentleman, I know for certain,' he went on in his ordinary voice, 'that when the Political Police Department sent for him, he grovelled at Countess Blazencrampf's feet and squeaked: "Save me, defend me!" And Pelikanov never sank to such baseness.'

' M-m-m. . . . Tenteleyev,' Gubaryov muttered. ' I must . . . I must make a note of that.'

Madame Suhanchikov contemptuously shrugged her shoulders.

' There's little to choose between them,' she began. ' But I know a better story than that about Tenteleyev. Everybody knows he was an awful tyrant to his serfs, though he pretended to support the emancipation. Well, one day he was at some friends' house in Paris, and suddenly Madame Beecher Stowe walked in—you know, *Uncle Tom's Cabin*. Tenteleyev, an awful snob, asked his host to introduce him; but as soon as she heard his name she said: "What? He dares to seek an introduction to the author of *Uncle Tom*?" And she gave him such a slap in the face! "Out you go," she said, "this very minute!" And what do you think? Tenteleyev took his hat and made off, his tail between his legs.'

' Oh, I think that's an exaggeration,' Bambaev remarked. ' She did say "Out you go," that's a fact; but she didn't slap his face.'

' She did, she did ! ' Madame Suhanchikov repeated with a kind of convulsive intensity. ' I am not one to talk nonsense ! And that's the sort of man you are friendly with ! '

' Come, come, Matryona Semyonovna, I never said Tenteleyev was my friend; I spoke of Pelikanov.'

' Well, if it isn't Tenteleyev, it's somebody of his sort: Mihnyov, for instance.'

' And what has Mihnyov done? ' asked Bambaev in alarm.

' What? Do you mean to say you don't know? He shouted in the Voznessensky Prospect for every one to hear that all the Liberals ought to be locked up; and another thing, an old school friend came to see him, a poor man, of course, and asked if he might stay to dinner, and Mihnyov said in reply: " No you can't; two counts are dining with me to-day . . . clear out ! "'

' But, goodness me, this is sheer slander ! ' Bambaev bellowed.

' Slander? Slander ? To begin with, Prince Vahrushkin who was also dining at your Mihnyov's——'

' Prince Vahrushkin,' Gubaryov sternly intervened, ' is my cousin, though I don't admit him into my presence. . . . So there's no occasion to mention him.'

'Secondly,' the lady went on, obediently inclining her head in Gubaryov's direction, ' Praskovya Yakovlevna told me herself.'

' Nice sort of authority ! She and Sarkizov are the greatest tale-tellers going ! '

' I beg your pardon ! Sarkizov certainly is a liar, and he did filch the brocade pall off his father's coffin,

21

I won't dispute that; but Praskovya Yakovlevna—
there's no comparison! Do you remember how nobly
she parted from her husband! But I know you are
always ready to——'

'Come, come, Matryona Semyonovna,' Bambaev
interrupted her. 'Let's stop squabbling and rise to
loftier regions! I am a chip of the old block, you
know. Have you read *Mlle de la Quintinie*? It's
really charming! And quite in keeping with your
principles!'

'I don't read novels any more,' the lady answered
dryly and incisively.

'Why not?'

'Because it isn't the time for it. I have only one
thing in my mind now: sewing machines.'

'What machines?' Litvinov asked.

'Sewing, sewing machines. All women must
provide themselves with them and form societies; in
this way they will all earn their living and become
independent at once. They can't gain freedom in
any other way. It's a most important social problem.
I had such an argument about it with Boleslav
Stadnitsky. Boleslav Stadnitsky is a beautiful character, but he is so thoughtless about those things.
He keeps laughing. . . . Idiot!'

'All shall be called to account in their time, all
shall have to answer,' Gubaryov uttered slowly in an
admonishing and prophetic tone.

'Yes, yes,' Bambaev repeated, 'called to account,
quite so. And what about your book, Stepan
Nicolaevitch,' he added in an undertone, 'how is it
getting on?'

'I am collecting materials,' Gubaryov answered with a frown, and turning to Litvinov, whose head was beginning to swim from this medley of unknown names and frenzied gossip, asked him what he was doing.

Litvinov satisfied his curiosity.

'Ah, natural science! It's useful as training; as training, but not as an end in itself. Our end at present should be . . . hm-m . . . should be . . . different. May I ask, what are your opinions?'

'What opinions?'

'That is, to be precise, what are your political convictions?'

Litvinov smiled.

'To be precise, I have no political convictions.'

At those words the thickset man in the corner suddenly raised his head and looked attentively at Litvinov.

'How is that?' Gubaryov inquired with strange mildness. 'Have you given no thought to the subject or wearied of it?'

'How shall I put it? It seems to me it is too soon for us Russians to have political convictions or to imagine that we have them. Mind, I use the word " political " in the sense which rightly belongs to it and——'

'Ah, still immature,' Gubaryov interrupted him with the same mildness, and going up to Voroshilov asked if he had read the pamphlet he lent him.

To Litvinov's surprise Voroshilov had not said a word since he came into the room, but merely frowned and significantly moved his eyes (as a general rule he either held forth at length or kept silence). He now thrust out his chest in military fashion, clicked his heels, and nodded.

'Well, did you approve of it?'

'I approve of the underlying principles, but I don't agree with the conclusions.'

'M-m-m. . . . But Andrey Ivanitch praised this pamphlet to me. Perhaps you will explain your doubts to me later.'

'Do you wish me to do it in writing?'

Gubaryov was obviously surprised: he had not expected it; but after thinking a little he said:

'Yes, in writing. By the way, I will also ask you to put down your ideas . . . about . . . about associations.'

'Would you have me do it on Lassalle's method or Schultze-Delitzsch's?'

'M-m-m . . . on both. You see, to us Russians it's the economic side that is of paramount importance. And, of course, the *artel*[1] . . . as the kernel. . . . It must all be taken into consideration. One must go into it thoroughly. And there's the question of the peasants' allotments. . . .'

'And how big do you, Stepan Nicolaevitch, think the allotments should be?' Voroshilov asked in a tone of deferential delicacy.

'M-m-m. . . . And the village commune?' Gubaryov uttered significantly and, taking a piece of his beard between his teeth, stared at the leg of the table. 'The commune. . . . Do you understand? It's a great word! And then, what is the meaning of those fires . . .

[1] Workers' association based on sharing both profits and responsibility. (Translator's note.)

24

of those . . . of those Government measures against
evening schools, reading-rooms, magazines? And of
the peasants' reluctance to sign settlement charters?
And, finally, think of what is happening in Poland. . . .
Don't you see what it's all leading to? Don't you see
that . . . m-m-m . . . that we . . . that we must now unite
with the people . . . learn . . . learn their opinion.'
Gubaryov was suddenly possessed by a kind of heavy
and almost spiteful emotion: a dark flush came into
his face and he breathed heavily, but he went on chewing his beard and did not raise his eyes. 'Don't you
see——?'

'Yevseyev is a scoundrel!' Madame Suhanchikov
blurted out suddenly; Bambaev had been telling her
something in an undertone out of respect for his
host. Gubaryov turned round sharply on his heels
and again began hobbling about the room.

New visitors appeared; towards the end of the
evening a good many people were assembled. Among
them was Mr. Yevseyev, so cruelly reviled by Madame
Suhanchikov; she talked to him quite amicably and
asked him to see her home. There came a certain
Pishchalkin, an ideal arbitrator of the peace,[1] one of
those men whom perhaps Russia really needs: a man
of limited intelligence, little knowledge, and no
talents, but honest, conscientious, and patient; the
peasants of his district simply worshipped him, and
he behaved with real deference to his own person, as
truly deserving of respect. Several young officers on
short leave to Europe came also, glad to have the

---

[1] Mediator between the gentry and the peasants during the
Emancipation period, an honorary post. (Translator's note.)

excitement of mixing with intellectual and slightly dangerous people, though of course with due care and bearing in mind their commanding officer. Two feeble-looking students from Heidelberg ran in; one kept looking about him contemptuously and the other laughed unnaturally . . . both felt very uncomfortable. They were followed by a Frenchman who somehow wormed himself into the room—a so-called *petit jeune homme*—a grubby young man, with neither money nor brains but renowned amongst his fellow commercial travellers for the fact that Russian countesses fell in love with him; he, however, was more concerned with getting a free supper. Finally Tit Bindasov came, in appearance a rowdy *Bursch* but in reality a bully and a skinflint, in words a terrorist, but by vocation a catchpoll, a friend of Russian merchants' wives and Parisian *cocottes*, bald, worthless, and drunk. He looked very flushed and repulsive, and assured every one that he had just lost his last farthing ' to that rascal Benazet,' though as a matter of fact he had won sixteen guldens. . . .

In short, there were a number of people. Remarkable, truly remarkable was the respect with which the visitors turned to Gubaryov as a master or chief. They put their doubts before him, submitting them to his judgment; and he answered by humming and hawing, pulling at his beard, rolling his eyes, or by insignificant, disconnected words which were immediately caught up as expressions of the loftiest wisdom. Gubaryov himself seldom took part in an argument, but the others did not spare their voices. It happened more than once that three or four shouted together for ten minutes at a time and all were perfectly content and understood one another. The conversation lasted till well after midnight and was marked as usual by the great range and variety of topics.

Madame Suhanchikov talked of Garibaldi, of a certain Karl Ivanovitch who had been flogged by his own house-serfs, of Napoleon III, of women's work, of a merchant called Pleskachov who, to everybody's knowledge, did to death twelve working-girls and was rewarded by a medal with the inscription ' for useful activities,' of the proletariat, of a Georgian prince, Chukcheulidzev, who had shot his wife with a cannon, and of Russia's future; Pishchalkin also spoke of Russia's future, of Government monopolies, of the significance of nationalities, and of how he hated the commonplace above all things. Voroshilov suddenly exploded, and in one breath, almost choking with words, he mentioned Draper, Virchow, Shelgunov, Bichat, Helmholtz, Star, Stur, Reimont, Johann Müller the physiologist, Johann Müller the historian, obviously confusing the two, Taine, Renan, Shchapov, and afterwards Thomas Nash, Peele, and Greene.

' What sort of birds are these? ' Bambaev muttered in surprise.

' Predecessors of Shakespeare who are in the same relation to him as the foothills of the Alps to Mont Blanc,' Voroshilov answered smartly—and he, too, touched on the future of Russia. Bambaev also spoke of Russia's future and described it in rainbow colours; he grew particularly enthusiastic at the thought of Russian music, in which he saw ' oh, something

27

great,' and as a proof began singing a song by Varla-mov—but was immediately interrupted by the general outcry that he was singing the 'Miserere' from *Il Trovatore* and singing it very badly too.

One of the young officers said, on the quiet, something abusive about Russian literature; another quoted a poem from *Iskra*.[1] Tit Bindasov was more straight-forward: he declared that all those rascals ought to have their teeth knocked out, and that's all about it—without explaining, however, who exactly those rascals were.

The smoke of the cigars was stifling; all were hot and torpid, all were hoarse, all eyes looked dull, all faces were bathed in perspiration. Bottles of cold beer were brought in and emptied instantly. 'What was I saying just now?' one person kept repeating. 'With whom was I arguing and what was it about?' another one was asking. And in the thick of all this hubbub Gubaryov walked about indefatigably, waddling as before and worrying his beard. He now turned an ear to listen to someone arguing, now put in a word of his own, and no one could help feeling that he, Gubaryov, was the head of it all, that he was the master and the chief person there. . . .

By about ten o'clock Litvinov developed a bad headache and slipped away unobserved, taking advantage of a fierce outburst of general shouting: Madame Suhanchikov recalled another outrage of Prince Barnaulov's—this time, it seems, he had given orders for someone's ear to be bitten off.

The fresh night air felt like a caress on Litvinov's

[1] A revolutionary magazine. (Translator's note.)

flushed face and poured into his parched lips like a fragrant stream.

'What is it,' he thought as he walked down the dark avenue of trees, 'I have been present at? What brought them together? Why did they shout, swear, work themselves up into a frenzy? What was it all for?'

Litvinov shrugged his shoulders and went to Weber's where he took up a newspaper and asked for an ice-cream. The newspaper discussed the problem of Rome, and the ice-cream was of poor quality. He was on the point of going home, when an unknown man wearing a wide-brimmed hat suddenly came up to him and, saying in Russian 'I hope I don't disturb you,' sat down at his table. It was only then that Litvinov, looking more closely at the stranger, recognized him as the thickset gentleman who had wedged himself into a corner in Gubaryov's room and scanned him so attentively when he spoke of political convictions. In the course of the whole evening this gentleman had not opened his mouth, and now, sitting down and taking off his hat, he looked at Litvinov with a friendly and rather shy expression in his eyes.

V

'Mr. Gubaryov, at whose rooms I had the pleasure
of seeing you to-day,' he began, 'did not introduce me
to you, so if I may, I'll do so myself: Potugin, retired
court councillor. I served in the Ministry of Finance
in Petersburg. I hope you will not find it strange. . . .
I am not in the habit of introducing myself so suddenly
. . . but in your case——'

Potugin hesitated and asked the waiter for a glass
of *Kirschwasser*. 'To buck me up,' he added with a
smile.

Litvinov looked with redoubled attention at his
new acquaintance, the last of those whom he had met
that day, and immediately said to himself, ' He is very
different.'

He certainly was different. The man who sat before
Litvinov, drumming with delicate fingers on the edge
of the table, was broad-shouldered, with a large body
on short legs, a downcast head of curly hair, very sad
and very intelligent eyes under bushy eyebrows, a
large, well-shaped mouth, bad teeth, and a purely
Russian ' potato-like' nose. He looked awkward
and even slightly uncouth, but he certainly was out of
the ordinary. He was carelessly dressed: his old-
fashioned frock-coat had a baggy look and his cravat
had slipped on to one side.

Far from regarding his sudden friendliness as an

impertinence, Litvinov was secretly flattered by it: it was obvious that this man was not in the habit of forcing himself upon strangers. He produced a strange impression on Litvinov, who felt respect and sympathy for him and at the same time a kind of involuntary pity.

'So I don't disturb you?' he repeated in a soft, weak voice that was slightly hoarse and quite in keeping with his whole figure.

'Not at all,' Litvinov replied. 'On the contrary, I am very glad.'

'Really? Well, then I am glad too. I've heard a great deal about you; I know what you are doing and what your plans are. It's a good work. No wonder you were silent to-night.'

'You didn't speak much either,' Litvinov remarked. Potugin gave a sigh.

'There was more than enough arguing going on. I listened. Well?' he added after a pause, with a humorous twist of his eyebrows, 'how did you like our babel?'

'That's just the word for it. You've put it admirably. I kept wanting to ask those people what all the fuss was about.'

Potugin sighed again.

'That's just the point—they don't know that themselves. In the old days they would have been described as "blind tools serving higher ends," but now we put it less politely. Mind you, I haven't the slightest intention of running them down; indeed, I will say that they are all...that is, almost all, excellent people. About Madame Suhanchikov, for instance, I know much that is really to her credit: she gave all the little money she had to her two poor nieces. And even if she did it partly from a desire to show off and cut a fine figure, anyway you will admit it meant wonderful self-sacrifice for a woman who is far from rich herself. As to Mr. Pishchalkin, there is simply no question: the peasants of his district will be sure to present him one day with a silver cup the shape of a water melon, or an ikon of his patron saint, and though he will say when he thanks them that he does not deserve such an honour, it won't be true: he does deserve it. Your friend Mr. Bambaev has a heart of gold; it's true, his enthusiasm is not directed to anything in particular—like the poet Yazykov's who is said to have sung the praises of revelry while reading a book and drinking water—but anyway, it is enthusiasm! Mr. Voroshilov, too, is a very good sort. Like all the young men of his type who have done brilliantly at school, he's been, so to speak, appointed an orderly to science and learning. His very silence is grandiloquent—but then he is so young! Yes, yes, they are all excellent people, and yet it does not come to anything. The ingredients are first rate, but the dish isn't fit to eat.'

Litvinov was more and more surprised as he listened to Potugin: the whole style of his leisurely and confident speech showed that he liked talking and was good at it.

That really was the case, but life had cured Potugin of vanity and he waited with philosophical calm for his opportunity, for a meeting with the right person.

'Yes, yes,' he began again with his peculiar, sad, but not jaundiced humour. 'It's all very strange.

And there's another thing I want you to note. If, for instance, ten Englishmen happen to meet together they'll begin talking about the submarine telegraph, the tax on paper, the method of tanning rats' skins—that is, of something practical and definite; if ten Germans meet, then of course Schleswig-Holstein and united Germany will appear on the scene; ten Frenchmen will inevitably end by talking about sex, avoid it as they will; but if ten Russians meet—you saw it for yourself to-day—they at once begin discussing the future and the significance of Russia, starting *ab ovo*, without any proofs or hope of coming to any conclusion. They chew and chew that unfortunate problem like children chewing a piece of rubber: no juice, no taste. And of course they'll have a dig at "the rotten West" by the way. It's a queer thing if you come to think of it—this West beats us on every point, and yet it's rotten! And it isn't as though we really had a contempt for it,' Potugin went on—'it's all mere talk and pretence. We certainly abuse the West, but its opinion is the only one we value—that is, at bottom, the opinion of Paris loafers. I know a man, a decent sort of fellow, no longer young, the father of a family; well, he spent several days in profound dejection because in a Paris restaurant he asked for *une portion de biftek aux pommes de terre*, and a real Frenchman at once called out "*Garçon! biftek pommes!*" My friend was simply withered with sham ! And afterwards he always shouted "*Biftek pommes!*" and taught others to do so. The *cocottes* themselves are surprised at the tremor of awe with which our young men from the steppes enter their shameful drawing-rooms. . . .

33

SMOKE

"Good heavens!" they say to themselves, "to think I am at Annah Deslions's house!"'

'Tell me, please,' Litvinov asked, 'how do you account for Gubaryov's unquestionable influence on all the others? Surely it's not because of any gifts or abilities?'

'Oh, no, he hasn't anything of that.'

'Is it his personal character, then?'

'No, it isn't that either, but he has plenty of will. As you know, we Slavs are not well off in that respect, and a strong will defeats us. Mr. Gubaryov wanted to be master, and every one has recognized him as such. What will you have? The Government has freed us from serfdom, all thanks be to it, but the habits of slavery are too deeply ingrained in us; it will take us years and years to get rid of them. Everywhere and in all things we want a master; as a rule that master is some actual person, though sometimes a so-called "tendency" gets the whip-hand of us—just now, for instance, we are all bondslaves of natural science.... Why we should enslave ourselves at all is a mystery; apparently, it's our nature. But the chief point is, we must have a master. Well, here we've got one: that means he is ours, and we don't care a button for all the rest. Regular flunkeys! Slavish pride and slavish self-abasement. A new master comes—down with the old one! The old one was Yakov, the new one is Sidor: box Yakov's ears and fall at Sidor's feet! Just recall things of that kind that happened amongst us! We say that the most characteristic thing about us is our critical spirit; but in our criticism we are not like a free man

striking with a sword but like a flunkey pummelling
with his fists—and very likely doing it at his master's
bidding.   And then, we are a soft people; it's easy
enough to take us in hand.   That's how Mr. Gubaryov
came to be master: he hammered and hammered at
one point till he got through.   People see a man has a
high opinion of himself, believes in himself, gives
orders—that's the chief thing, gives orders!—so they
conclude he must be right and should be obeyed.
That's just how all our Dissenters' sects arose—all our
Onuphrists and Akulinists.   Whoever takes up the
stick is master.'

A flush came into Potugin's cheeks and his eyes
grew dim; but strange to say, his words, bitter and
even spiteful, had no touch of venom in them but
rather of sorrow—real, genuine sorrow.

' How did you come to know Gubaryov? ' Litvinov
asked.

' Oh, I've known him for years.   And note another
curious thing about us: an author or someone of that
sort, for instance, may spend his life denouncing
drunkenness in prose and verse and attacking the
drink monopoly, and then suddenly go and buy two
distilleries and rent a hundred drink-shops—and nobody minds!   Another man would have been ground
off the face of the earth, but he is not even criticized.
Take Mr. Gubaryov now: he is a Slavophil and a
democrat and a socialist and everything you like, but
his estate has always been, and still is, managed by
his brother, a landowner of the old school—one of
those who are free with their fists.   And Madame
Suhanchikov, who makes Mrs. Beecher Stowe box

Tenteleyev's ears, simply grovels before Gubaryov. But all that there is to him is that he reads serious books and plunges into the depths. What his gift of speech is, you could judge for yourself to-day; and it's just as well that he says little and merely bristles. When he is in good spirits and lets himself go, even a patient man like me can't stand it. He makes jokes and tells smutty stories—yes, yes, our great Mr. Gubaryov tells smutty stories, and laughs at them in such a disgusting way.'

'Are you so patient as all that?' Litvinov asked. 'I would have thought, on the contrary—— But allow me to ask your name.'

Potugin took a few sips of *Kirschwasser*.

'I am called Sozont—Sozont Ivanitch. That beautiful name was given me in honour of a relative, an archimandrite, to whom I am not indebted in any other way. I come of priestly stock, if I may put it so. But you needn't doubt my patience: I am very patient. I served for twenty-two years under my own uncle, an actual civil councillor, Irinark Potugin. You haven't met him, have you?'

'No.'

'Lucky for you. Yes, I am patient. But "let us return to the first," as my respected *confrère*, Archpriest Avvakum,[1] burnt at the stake, used to say. I marvel at my compatriots, my dear sir. They are all downcast, they are all a picture of dejection, and at the same time they are full of hope and at the least provocation go simply wild. Take the Slavophils, for instance,

---

[1] Leader of the 'Old Believers' in the seventeenth century. (Translator's note.)

36

to whom Mr. Gubaryov is supposed to belong; most excellent people, but it's the same mixture of despair and defiance, the same " living in the future." It will all come, they say. At the moment there is nothing at all, and in the course of ten centuries Russia has produced nothing of its own either in government or in law or in science or in art, or even in crafts. . . . But wait, have patience—it will all come. Why will it all come, may I ask? Because we educated people are poor stuff, but the people . . . oh, it's a great people! Look at the peasant! That's where it will all come from. All other idols have been shattered, so let us believe in the peasant. And what if he fails us? Oh, no, he won't; read Madame Kohanovsky and raise your eyes up to heaven! Really, if I were a painter, this is the picture I'd draw: an educated man is standing before a peasant and saying to him with a low bow: " Cure me, my good man, I am perishing of disease"; and the peasant in his turn bows low to the educated man and says: "Teach me, good sir, I am perishing of ignorance." And of course neither stirs an inch. But all that's needed is to be truly humble— not in words only—and borrow from our elder brothers what they have invented before us and better than us. *Köllner, noch ein Gläschen Kirsch!* Don't think I am a drunkard, but alcohol loosens my tongue.'

' After what you've just said,' Litvinov said with a smile, ' I needn't ask to what party you belong and what you think of Europe. But allow me to make one remark to you. You say we ought to borrow from our elder brothers and imitate them; but how can one borrow without taking into consideration the

37

climate, the soil, the local and national peculiarities? I remember, my father ordered from Butenop's a cast-iron winnowing machine, highly advertised and really excellent, but what happened? It stood for five years in the barn unused and then was replaced by a wooden American one, which is much better suited to our ways and habits, as indeed all American machines are. It's no use borrowing thoughtlessly, Sozont Ivanitch.'

Potugin raised his head.

'I didn't expect such an argument from you, my dear Grigory Mihailovitch,' he began after a pause. 'Why ever should you borrow thoughtlessly? You take foreign things not because they are foreign but because they suit you: that is, you use your judgment, you choose. And don't you trouble about the results: they'll have a character of their own right enough, just because of those local and climatic conditions you mention. All you have to do is to offer good food, and the national stomach will digest it in its own way; and in time, when the organism grows strong, it will give it a flavour of its own. Take our language, for instance. Peter the Great flooded it with thousands of foreign words, Dutch, French, German: those words expressed ideas to which the Russian people had to be introduced. Without ceremony or meaning Peter poured them wholesale into us by bucketfuls and barrelfuls. At first the result certainly was something monstrous, but then there began that very process of digestion of which I was speaking. The ideas struck root and became assimilated; foreignisms gradually disappeared, the language found forms of its own by which to replace them—and now your humble servant, by no means a master of style, would undertake to translate any page you like out of Hegel —yes, yes, out of Hegel!—without using a single non-Slavonic word. The same thing that has happened with the language will, let us hope, happen in other spheres. The whole point is whether one's constitution is strong enough, and I don't think we need worry about ours: we've been through worse plights than that. Only neurotic people and feeble nations can fear for their health and independence; just as it is only idle people who can fall into raptures at the fact that we are Russians. I am very careful about my health, but I don't go into ecstasies about it—I would be ashamed.'

' That's all very well, Sozont Ivanitch,' Litvinov said in his turn, 'but why subject us to such trials? You say yourself that the result was at first something monstrous! And what if the monstrosity had remained? And, indeed, it has remained, you know it yourself.'

' But not in language—and that means a great deal! Well, it isn't I who made our nation; it isn't my fault that it is destined to pass through such a school. The Germans have developed in a normal way. The Slavophils cry: " Give us the same kind of development! " But how is that to be done when the very first historical action of our people—the calling of princes from overseas to rule over them—is irregular and abnormal? And it is repeated in every one of us to this day; every one of us, if only once in his life, is certain to have said to something that is foreign, not Russian: " Come and rule over me." I am ready to admit, if you like, that in putting foreign substance into our own body we can't possibly know beforehand whether it will prove to be bread or poison; but then we all know that the way from bad to good is never through " better," but always through " worse "—and even poison is useful in medicine. Only fools or knaves can point with triumph to the peasants' poverty after the emancipation and to their drinking more since the farming of the spirit tax was abolished. . . . Through worse to better!'

Potugin passed his hand over his face.

' You asked me what I think of Europe,' he began again. ' I admire it and am wholly devoted to its principles, and don't see the slightest necessity to conceal this. I have long—no, not so very long— it's some time since I lost the fear of saying what I really think. . . . I saw, you too didn't hesitate to tell Mr. Gubaryov what your views are. Thank heaven, I no longer try to accommodate myself to the ideas, beliefs, and habits of the person to whom I am talking. I really know nothing worse than the needless cowardice, the wretched obsequiousness which sometimes makes an important official play up to some insignificant student, and try to ingratiate himself with him. Well, an official may do so for the sake of being popular, but why should plain men like us prevaricate? Yes, I am a Westernizer and am devoted to Europe— or, rather, I am devoted to culture, to that very culture which is now the subject of such charming jokes among us, to civilization—yes, that's a better word— I love it with all my heart and believe in it. I have no other faith and never shall have. That word, ci-vi-li-za-tion' (Potugin laid emphasis on every syllable as he said it) 'is intelligible, and pure and holy, while all other—nationality, glory, and the rest of it, smell of blood . . . better leave them alone!'

'And do you love Russia, your motherland, Sozont Ivanitch?'

Potugin passed his hand over his face.

'I love it passionately, and hate it passionately too.'

Litvinov shrugged his shoulders.

'That's old, Sozont Ivanitch, that's commonplace.'

'Well, what of it? What's wrong with it? Fancy being afraid of commonplaces! I know many good commonplaces. For instance, freedom and order is a well-known one. Do you think it's better to have it our way—bureaucratic tyranny and disorder? And, besides, all those phrases that turn so many young heads—"contemptible bourgeoisie," *souveraineté du peuple*, the right to work—are commonplaces too. And as to love inseparable from hate——'

'Byronism,' Litvinov interrupted, 'romanticism of the thirties.'

'You are mistaken, excuse me; the first to point out that mixture of feelings was Catullus,[1] the Roman poet Catullus, two thousand years ago. I read it in his poems because I know some Latin, thanks to my clerical origin, if I may put it so. Yes, I both love and hate Russia, my strange, charming, disgusting, and precious motherland. I have left it for the moment: I had to have an airing after sitting for twenty years at an office desk in a government building; I have

[1] Odi et amo. Quare id faciam, fortasse, requiris?
Nescio; sed fieri sentio et excrucior.
Catullus, lxxxv.

41

left Russia and I enjoy being here very much, but I feel I shall soon go back.   Garden soil is fine . . . but it's not the soil for cranberries ! '

' You enjoy being here, and so do I,' said Litvinov, ' and I've come here as a learner; but that doesn't prevent my seeing this sort of thing, for instance . . .' he pointed to two passing *cocottes* surrounded by several members of the Jockey Club affecting to speak Parisian French, and to the gambling-hall, crowded in spite of the late hour.

' And why do you suppose I am blind to it? ' Potugin retorted.   ' But, excuse me, your remark reminds me of the jubilations of our miserable press during the Crimean War over the defects of the English War Office pointed out by *The Times*.   I am not an optimist and I don't see in a rosy light either human nature or life as a whole—all this comedy with a tragic ending— but why ascribe to the West what may be rooted in human essence as such?   This gambling-hall is hideous certainly, but are our home-grown card-sharpers any better?   No, my dear Grigory Mihailo- vitch, let's be more humble and quiet: a good pupil sees his master's faults, but keeps respectfully silent about them, for those very faults are of benefit to him and help him to keep straight.   And if you want to have a dig at the "rotten West," here is Prince Kokó trotting along; he has probably lost during a quarter of an hour at the gambling-table the tax wrung out of a hundred and fifty hard-working peasant families, and his nerves are unstrung; besides, I saw him to-day at Marx's turning the pages of Veuillot's pamphlet. . . . He'll be an excellent person for you to talk to ! '

' But I say ! ' Litvinov said hastily, seeing that Potugin was getting up. ' I hardly know Prince Kokó, and in any case I much prefer talking to you——'

' Thank you very much,' Potugin interrupted him, getting up and bowing, ' but we've had quite a long talk, or rather it was I who talked all the time. You probably know from your own experience that a man always feels awkward and a bit ashamed when he has done all the talking. Especially on a first meeting: as though he meant to show what a fine fellow he is ! Good-bye for the present. And I repeat, I am very glad to have met you.'

' But wait a minute, Sozont Ivanitch, tell me at any rate where you live and how long you are staying here?'

Potugin looked slightly uncomfortable.

' I shall be at Baden for another week, but we can meet here, at Weber's or at Marx's. Or I'll call on you.'

' But all the same I'd like to have your address.'

' Yes. But, you see, I am not alone.'

' Are you married?' Litvinov asked suddenly.

' Dear me, no. What a queer idea ! But I have a young lady with me.'

' Ah !' Litvinov said with a polite expression, as though apologizing, and lowered his eyes.

' She is only six,' Potugin went on. ' She is an orphan—the daughter of a lady . . . who was a friend of mine. It will be better for us to meet here. Good-bye.'

He pulled his hat over his curly head of hair and rapidly disappeared. Litvinov caught one or two glimpses of him under the gas lamps that shed rather a scanty light on the road leading to the Lichtenthal Avenue.

VI

' A STRANGE man ! ' thought Litvinov on the way to
his hotel. ' A strange man ! I must look him up.'

He went into his room; a letter on the table caught
his eye. ' Ah, from Tanya ! ' he thought joyfully;
but the letter proved to be from his father in the country. Litvinov broke the large crested seal and began
reading. . . . A strong, very pleasant and familiar
smell attracted his attention. He turned round and
saw a large bouquet of fresh heliotrope in a tumbler
of water in the window. Litvinov bent down to the
flowers with some surprise, touched them, sniffed
them. . . . They seemed to remind him of something . . .
of something very remote; but what it was he could
not think. He rang for the servant and asked where
the flowers had come from. The man answered that
they had been brought by a lady who would not give
her name but said that he, ' Herr Zluitenhof,' would
be sure to guess from those flowers who she was.
Litvinov again seemed to recall something. . . . He
asked the servant what the lady looked like. The man
explained that she was tall and beautifully dressed and
wore a veil over her face.

' Probably a Russian countess,' he added.

' What makes you think that ? ' Litvinov asked.

' She gave me two guldens,' the man answered with a
grin. Litvinov dismissed him and for a few minutes

stood by the window, thinking; but at last he gave it up as hopeless and again began reading the letter from the country. His father poured out in it his usual complaints, assured him that no one wanted corn even as a gift, that servants had lost all habit of obedience, and that probably the end of the world was at hand. ' Would you believe it,' he wrote among other things, ' they cast a spell over my last coachman, the little Calmuck, you remember? The man would certainly have died and I should have been left without a coachman, but fortunately kind people gave me the tip and advised me to send the invalid to Ryazan, to a priest who is a master hand at curing such cases. And he really did cure my man, in confirmation of which I enclose the reverend father's own letter as documentary proof.' Litvinov read the document with much interest. It said that ' a former house serf, Nikanor Dmitriev, was ill of a disease inaccessible to medical science; the disease was due to evil people, but the cause of it was Nikanor himself because he had failed to carry out his promise to a certain young woman; and she, through the aid of others, made him unfit for anything; and if I hadn't been here to help him he would have perished like a miserable worm; but, trusting to the All-seeing Eye, I came to his rescue; how I did it is a secret; but I ask your honour to tell the young woman not to venture upon such evil deeds in the future, and it would be a good thing to threaten her or else she may do mischief to him again.'

Litvinov pondered deep over that document; it seemed to have brought with it a breath of the blind darkness and the stagnant life in the wild steppes, and it was queer that he should be reading it at Baden of all places. Meanwhile it had long struck midnight; Litvinov got into bed and blew out his candle. But he could not go to sleep; the people he had met, the phrases he had heard kept coming back and circling round in strange and confused combinations in his burning head that ached with the tobacco smoke. At times he fancied he heard Gubaryov mumbling and saw the dull and obstinate look in his downcast eyes; then suddenly those eyes grew bright and restless and he recognized Madame Suhanchikov, heard her strident voice, and involuntarily repeated after her in a whisper: ' She did box his ears, she did'; then Potugin's unwieldy figure rose before him and he recalled for the tenth and the twentieth time every word he had said; Voroshilov jumped out like a jack-in-the-box in his tight-fitting overcoat that looked like a new uniform; Pishchalkin wisely and pompously nodded his well-trimmed and truly well-intentioned head; Bindasov shouted and swore, and Bambaev went into tearful raptures. . . . But, above all, that clinging, sweet, heavy fragrance gave him no peace. It seemed to grow more and more intense in the darkness, and to remind him more and more insistently of something he could not recall. . . . It occurred to Litvinov that the scent of flowers in the bedroom was bad for one at night; he got up, fumbled his way to the bouquet, and carried it into the adjoining room, but the languorous fragrance penetrated from there to his pillow, stole under the bedclothes, and he tossed miserably from side to side. Feverish dreams were gaining hold of him; the priest, ' a master hand against witchcraft,' in the guise of a very nimble hare with a beard and a plait of hair ran twice across his path; Voroshilov, sitting in a huge general's cockade as in a bush, sang like a nightingale before him . . . when suddenly he sat up in bed and cried out, clasping his hands:

' Can it be *she*?   Surely not ! '

But in order to explain Litvinov's exclamation we must ask the indulgent reader to go with us a few years back.

VII

In the early fifties there lived in Moscow in very straitened circumstances, not to say in poverty, the numerous family of the Princes Osinin. They were not Tatar or Georgian but real princes descended from Ryurik; their name often occurs in our chronicles under the first Grand Princes of Moscow, 'the gatherers of the Russian land.' They had possessed large hereditary domains, were more than once rewarded for 'service and blood and wounds,' sat in the Boyar Duma, and one of them actually had the privilege of using his patronymic in full. But they fell into disfavour through their enemies accusing them of 'witchcraft and sorcery'; they were ruined 'terribly and completely,' deprived of honours, and sent into exile. The Osinins fell never to rise again; in time they were reinstated in the Tsar's favour and had their Moscow house and belongings restored to them, but it was of no avail. Having once sunk into poverty they did not make good either under Peter or under Catherine; sinking lower and lower in the social scale, the family reckoned among its members stewards of private estates, chiefs of distilleries, and district police officers.

The Osinin household to which we have referred consisted of husband, wife, and five children. They lived near Dogs' Square in a wooden one-storeyed house with a striped front porch, green lions on the gates, and other pretensions of nobility, and could barely make ends meet, owed money to their green-grocer, and in winter were often without candles or fuel. The prince was a dull and sluggish man; in his youth he had been handsome and a dandy, but had let himself go completely. Out of consideration for his wife, who had been a maid-of-honour, rather than out of respect for his ancient name, he was given one of the old-fashioned Moscow government posts with a small salary, a high-sounding name, and nothing whatever to do. He did not interfere in anything and spent the days wrapped in his dressing-gown, smoking from morning to night and sighing heavily. His wife was a sick and embittered woman perpetually worried over domestic troubles, over placing her children in government schools, and keeping up her Petersburg connections. She could not reconcile herself to her position and to losing touch with the court.

When Litvinov's father was in Moscow he met the Osinins, had occasion to do them a few services, and once lent them three hundred roubles; his son in his student days often came to see them; his lodgings happened to be not far from their house. But he was drawn to them not because they were neighbours or because their poor way of living attracted him: he began frequenting them after he had fallen in love with their eldest daughter Irina.

She was seventeen at the time; she had just left an aristocratic boarding-school from which her mother took her away through an unpleasantness with the headmistress. The unpleasantness was due to the fact that on the school leaving day Irina was to have recited in French congratulatory verses to the chairman of the School Board, but just before the ceremony she was replaced by another pupil, the daughter of a very rich spirit-contractor. The princess could not get over such a slight, and Irina herself did not forgive the headmistress for her unfairness. She had been dreaming how in the sight of all, attracting general attention, she would get up and recite her verses, and how Moscow would talk of her afterwards. . . .

And indeed, Moscow would probably have talked of Irina. She was a tall, graceful girl with the narrow shoulders of youth and a slightly flat chest; marble-white skin, rare at her age, pure and smooth like porcelain, and a mass of fair hair, in which the darker strands curiously alternated with the light one. Her features, exquisitely, almost faultlessly regular, had not yet completely lost the simple-hearted expression natural to early youth, but the languid droop of her pretty neck and her smile, dreamy or indifferent, suggested a temperamental young lady; and in the curves of those fine, faintly smiling lips and of the small, rather narrow aquiline nose there was something passionate and self-willed, something dangerous both for herself and for others. Wonderful, truly wonderful were her eyes, soft and dreamy, shaped like the eyes of Egyptian goddesses, dark grey with a tinge of green, with long eyelashes and boldly shaped eyebrows. There was a strange expression in those eyes: they seemed to gaze attentively and thoughtfully out of some mysterious depth and distance.

At school Irina was one of the best pupils for

intelligence and ability, but was reputed to be change-able, imperious, and reckless. One of the mistresses told her that her passions would be the ruin of her— '*vos passions vous perdront*,' but another one accused her of coldness and insensibility and called her '*une jeune fille sans cœur*.' Irina's school friends found her proud and secretive, her brothers and sisters stood rather in awe of her, her mother distrusted her, and her father felt uncomfortable when she fixed her mysterious eyes on him; but she inspired both her father and mother with involuntary respect, not because of her character but because of peculiar vague expectations which she somehow aroused in them.

' You'll see, Praskovya Danilovna,' the old prince said one day taking his pipe out of his mouth, ' that girl will give us a leg up one day.'

The princess was angry and said to her husband that he had '*des expressions insupportables*,' but then she pondered and muttered through her teeth:

' Yes . . . and it would be a good thing, too.'

Irina enjoyed almost unlimited freedom in her parents' house; they did not spoil her and indeed held rather aloof from her, but they did not thwart her, and that was all she wanted. When something particularly humiliating happened—when one of the tradesmen came and shouted all over the yard that he was tired of coming after his own money, or the servants began abusing their masters to their faces and saying it wasn't much good their being princes if they hadn't a crust to bite—Irina did not stir an eyelid but sat motionless with a malicious smile on her gloomy

51

face; yet to her parents that smile was more bitter than any reproaches. They felt guilty—though they had done her no wrong—towards this girl who seemed to have been given from birth the right to wealth, luxury, and admiration.

Litvinov fell in love with Irina at first sight (he was only three years older than she), but it took him a long time to attract her attention, let alone win her love. Her manner to him had a trace of strange hostility: it was as though he had offended her and she had deeply concealed the injury but could not forgive it. He was too young and modest at the time to understand what might have been hidden under that hostile, almost contemptuous harshness. Forgetting his lectures and note-books he would often sit in the depressing drawing-room of the Osinins, secretly watching Irina; his heart slowly and painfully melting within him was like a heavy weight in his breast; and she looked as though she were angry or bored; she would get up and walk across the room, look at him coldly as on a piece of furniture, shrug her shoulders, and fold her arms. Or during the whole evening, even while talking to Litvinov, she would not once look at him, as though refusing him even that favour; or she would open a book and, not reading, stare at it frowning and biting her lips; or she would suddenly ask aloud her father or brother what was the German for patience.

He tried to break away from the enchanted circle in which he suffered and struggled helplessly like a bird in a trap; he left Moscow for a week. He nearly went mad with longing and misery, and thin and ill, returned to the Osinins. . . . Curiously enough, Irina too had grown noticeably thinner during that week, her face had a yellowish tinge, her cheeks had lost their roundness—but she met him even more coldly than usual, with an almost malicious negligence, as though he had somehow aggravated the secret injury he had done to her. . . . She tormented him in that way for a couple of months. Then it all suddenly changed in one day. Love flared up like a flame, came upon them like a thunderstorm. Once again—he remembered that day for years—he was sitting in the Osinins' drawing-room by the window, looking blankly into the street; he was vexed and bored and full of contempt for himself, and yet he could not move from his chair. He fancied that if a river flowed there, by the window, he would jump into it with horror, but without regret. Irina sat not far from him, strangely silent and still. She had not spoken to him or indeed to any one for several days; she sat leaning her head on her hand as though in perplexity and sometimes slowly looked round her. At last Litvinov could stand this cold anguish no longer; he got up and without saying good-bye began looking for his hat.

'Stay,' he suddenly heard a soft whisper.

Litvinov's heart quivered, he did not at once recognize Irina's voice: a note he had never heard sounded in that word. He raised his head and was dumbfounded: Irina was looking at him kindly—yes, she really was.

'Stay,' she repeated, 'don't go. I want to be with you.' She lowered her voice. 'Don't go—I don't want you to.'

Understanding nothing, scarcely knowing what he

was doing, he came up to her and held out his
hands. She at once gave him both hers, smiled,
flushed crimson, turned away and, still smiling, went
out of the room. . . . A few minutes later she returned
with her younger sister, looked at him again with the
same gentle gaze, and made him sit down beside her.
At first she could say nothing, and only sighed and
blushed; then she began shyly asking him about his
work, which she had never done before.

In the evening of that same day she asked him
several times to forgive her for not having recognized
his worth before, assured him that now she was quite
different, and surprised him by a sudden republican
sally (at that time he revered Robespierre and did not
venture openly to condemn Marat). A week later
he knew that she loved him.

Yes, he long remembered that first day . . . but he
had not forgotten the days that came after, when, still
trying to doubt and afraid to believe, he clearly saw
with a thrill of rapture and almost of awe how the
unexpected happiness arose, grew, and sweeping everything before it, flooded his heart at last. There
followed the radiant moments of first love, which are
not, and indeed ought not to be, repeated in the same
life. Irina suddenly became gentle as a lamb, soft as
silk, and infinitely kind; she began giving lessons to
her younger sisters in French and in English—she did
not teach them the piano for she was no musician—
read their school books with them, occupied herself
with housekeeping; everything amused her, everything
interested her. She either chattered unceasingly or
sank into a mood of silent tenderness. She made

plans, indulged in endless schemes of what she would do when she married Litvinov (they had not the slightest doubt that their marriage would come to pass), of how, together, they would ... 'Work?' Litvinov prompted her ... 'Yes, work,' Irina repeated, 'read ... but above all, travel.' She was particularly anxious to leave Moscow as soon as possible, and when Litvinov pointed out to her that he had not yet graduated she replied every time, after thinking a little, that he could finish his studies in Berlin—or somewhere.

Irina did not take much trouble to conceal her feelings, and accordingly her attachment to Litvinov soon ceased to be a secret for her parents. They were not overjoyed, but taking everything into consideration did not think it necessary to impose their veto at once. Litvinov was quite well off. . . .

'But the name, the name!' the princess remarked.

'Well, of course,' the prince answered, 'but anyway he is a gentleman, and the chief point is, Irina wouldn't obey us, you know. She has never failed to do what she had set her heart on. *Vous connaissez sa violence!* And besides, there's nothing definite as yet.'

That was what the prince said, but he added in his mind: 'Madame Litvinov—and that's all! I expected something different.'

Irina took complete possession of Litvinov, and he readily surrendered himself to her. It was as though he had fallen into a whirlpool, as though he had lost himself ... it was frightening and sweet, and there was nothing he regretted, nothing that he held back. He could not reflect about the significance and the duties of marriage, or decide whether a man so completely subjugated as he was would make a good husband, and what sort of wife Irina would be, and whether they stood in the right relation to each other; his blood was on fire and all he knew was that he must follow her, be with her, go on and on, come what may! But in spite of all absence of resistance on Litvinov's part and Irina's overflowing impulsive tenderness, there were a few jolts and misunderstandings between them.   One day he ran in to the Osinins' straight from the university, in an old jacket, his hands stained with ink.   She rushed to meet him with her usual warm welcome and suddenly drew back.

' You have no gloves,' she said slowly, and added at once: 'fie, you are a regular—student! '

' You are too impressionable, Irina.'

' You are—a regular student,' she repeated. *Vous n'êtes pas distingué.*' And turning her back on him she went out of the room.   True, an hour later she implored him to forgive her. . . .   As a rule she readily repented and asked his forgiveness, but, strange to say, she often accused herself almost with tears of bad motives that were purely imaginary and obstinately denied her real failings.

On another occasion he found her in tears, her head in her hands and her hair loose.   When he asked in alarm what was troubling her she silently pointed with her finger at her bosom.   Litvinov shuddered. ' Consumption! ' flashed through his mind and he seized her hand.

' Are you ill? ' he said in an unsteady voice.   ' I'll run for the doctor at once——'

But Irina stamped her foot in vexation, not letting him finish.

'I am perfectly well . . . but this dress—don't you understand?'

'What is it—"this dress . . ."' he repeated in perplexity.

'What is it? Why, that I have no other, that it's old and horrid and yet I have to wear it every day even—even when you come. You'll fall out of love with me at last, seeing me so dowdy!'

'Good heavens, Irina, what are you saying! And it is a charming dress. I am fond of it, too, because you wore it when I first saw you.'

Irina blushed.

'Don't remind me, please, Grigory Mihailovitch, that I hadn't another dress even then.'

'But I assure you, it suits you beautifully.'

'No, it's horrid, horrid,' she repeated, nervously pulling at her long, soft curls. 'Oh, this poverty, this squalor! How is one to escape it? How to get out of the squalor?'

Litvinov did not know what to say and turned slightly away. Suddenly Irina jumped up from her chair and put both her hands on his shoulders.

'But you love me? You love me?' she said, bringing her face near to his, and her eyes, still full of tears, sparkled with the joy of happiness. 'You love me even in this horrid dress?'

Litvinov fell at her feet.

'Ah, love me, love me, my dear one, my saviour,' she whispered bending over him.

In this way days flew by, weeks passed. There had

been no formal explanations, Litvinov still delayed with his proposal—not of his own wish, of course, but waiting for a word from Irina (she had remarked one day that they were both ridiculously young, and ought to add at least a few more weeks to their years)— but everything was moving towards the conclusion, and the immediate future was shaping itself more and more clearly. Suddenly an event took place which scattered all their dreams and plans like light wayside dust.

VIII

THAT winter the court visited Moscow. One series of festivities followed another; at last the time came for the customary big ball at the Hall of Nobility. The news of this ball reached even the house in Dogs' Square,—though only, it is true, in the form of an advertisement in the *Police Gazette*. The prince was the first to take it to heart; he at once decided that they must certainly go and take Irina, that it would be unpardonable to miss an opportunity of seeing one's sovereign, and that indeed it was a kind of duty for the old nobility. He insisted on this with a fervour not at all natural to him; the princess agreed with him up to a point and only sighed over the expense; but Irina was dead against it. 'There's no need to, I won't go,' she replied to all her parents' arguments. Her obstinacy was so unmanageable that the old prince decided at last to ask Litvinov to try to persuade her, giving her among other reasons that it was absurd for a young girl to fight shy of society, that ' she ought to have the experience,' and that no one saw her anywhere, as it was. Litvinov agreed to put these arguments before her. Irina looked at him closely and attentively—so closely and attentively that he felt uncomfortable—and, playing with the ends of her waistband, asked calmly:

' Do you wish it? You?'

'Yes . . . I think,' Litvinov faltered, 'I agree with your father. And why shouldn't you go . . . to have a look at people and show yourself?' he added with a short laugh.

'Show myself?' she repeated slowly. 'Very well, I'll go. . . . But remember, it was you who wished it.'

'That is, I——' Litvinov began.

'You yourself have wished it,' she interrupted him. 'And one condition more: you must promise me that you won't be at the ball.'

'But why?'

'I don't want you to.'

Litvinov threw up his hands.

'I obey . . . but I confess I would so have enjoyed seeing you in all your splendour and watching the impression you are bound to produce. . . . How proud I would be of you!' he added with a sigh.

Irina smiled.

'All my splendour will consist of a white frock, and as to the impression—— Well, anyway, I don't want you to be there.'

'Irina, you seem to be angry?'

Irina smiled again.

'Oh, no! I am not angry. Only——' She fixed her eyes on him, and he thought he had never seen such an expression in them. 'Perhaps it has to be,' she added in an undertone.

'But do you love me, Irina?'

'I love you,' she answered almost solemnly and pressed his hand firmly, like a man.

During the days that followed, Irina took great

60

interest in her dress and the way she did her hair; on the eve of the ball she felt unwell, could not sit still, wept once or twice when she was alone; in Litvinov's presence she smiled a kind of fixed smile. She was as tender with him as ever, but she was absent-minded and continually glanced at herself in the mirror. On the actual day of the ball she was very silent and pale, but calm. About nine o'clock in the evening Litvinov came to have a look at her. When she appeared before him in a white muslin dress, with a spray of small blue flowers in her slightly raised hair, he almost cried out: so beautiful she seemed to him and so stately, quite beyond her years. 'Yes, she has grown up since this morning,' he thought, 'and what a bearing she has! Race does mean something after all!'

Irina stood before him without smiling or looking self-conscious, her hands hanging loose. She gazed resolutely, almost defiantly, not at him but straight before her into the distance.

'You are like a princess in a fairy tale,' Litvinov said at last, 'or, no: you are like a commander before a victorious battle.... You wouldn't allow me to go to this ball,' he went on while she stood motionless as before and seemed to be listening not to him, but to some other, inner voice, 'but I hope you won't refuse to accept these flowers and take them with you?'

He gave her a bouquet of heliotrope.

She glanced at him quickly, stretched out her hand and said, suddenly seizing the end of the spray which adorned her head:

'Would you have me stay? At a word from you I'll tear it all off and stay at home.'

Litvinov's heart gave a jump. Irina's hand was already tearing off the spray.

'No, no, why should you,' he answered hurriedly in an excess of generous and grateful feelings. 'I am not an egoist, why interfere with your liberty . . . when I know that your heart——'

'Well then, don't come near, you'll crumple my dress,' she said hastily.

Litvinov was taken aback.

'And will you take the bouquet?' he asked.

'Of course: it's charming and I am very fond of that scent. *Merci* . . . I'll keep it in memory of——'

'Your first ball,' Litvinov remarked, 'your first triumph.'

Turning slightly, Irina looked at herself in the mirror over her shoulder.

'And do I really look so nice? You are not flattering me?'

Litvinov went off into enthusiastic praises. But Irina was not listening to him; holding the flowers up to her face she was again gazing into the far distance with her strange eyes that seemed to have grown darker and bigger, and the ends of her soft ribbons, disturbed by the slight current of air, rose behind her shoulders like wings.

The prince made his appearance in a white tie and a faded black tail-coat; his hair was curled and he wore the medal of nobility on a Vladimir ribbon in the lapel of his coat. The princess, wearing an old-fashioned silk gown, followed him into the room. With the air of stern solicitude under which mothers try to hide their agitation she put her daughter to rights at the back,

that is, quite unnecessarily shook the folds of her dress. A hired closed carriage for four, drawn by two shaggy hacks, crawled up to the front porch; a puny footman in a queer kind of livery popped his head in at the drawing-room door, and with a certain recklessness in his voice declared that the carriage was ready. Having blessed for the night the children left at home, the prince and princess put on their fur coats and went out on to the steps; Irina silently followed them wrapped in a thin and short cloak—how she hated that cloak! Litvinov, who was seeing them off, had hoped that Irina would give him a parting look, but she stepped into the carriage without turning her head.

About midnight he walked past the windows of the Hall of Nobility. Innumerable lights of huge candelabras showed like bright specks through the red window-curtains and the strains of a Strauss waltz floated festively, insolently, and defiantly over the square blocked with carriages.

The next day Litvinov went to the Osinins' soon after twelve o'clock. The only person to receive him was the prince, who immediately informed him that Irina had a headache and would stay in bed all day, which indeed was not at all surprising after a first ball. ' C'est très naturel, vous savez, dans les jeunes filles,' he added in French, which rather surprised Litvinov who instantly noticed that the prince was wearing a frock-coat instead of his usual dressing-gown. ' And besides,' Osinin went on, ' she might well be ill after all the events of last night! '

' Events? ' Litvinov muttered.

63

'Yes, yes, events, *de vrais événements*. You can't imagine, Grigory Mihailovitch, *quel succès elle a eu*! The whole court noticed her. Prince Alexandr Fyodorovitch said that her place was not here and that she reminded him of the Duchess of Devonshire . . . you know . . . the famous one. And old Blazen-crampf declared aloud that Irina was *la reine du bal*, and asked to be introduced to her; he introduced himself to me too, that is, he told me he remembered me as a hussar and asked what I was doing now. He is most amusing, that count, and such an *adorateur du beau sexe*! But not only me—they wouldn't leave even my wife in peace: Natalya Nikitishna herself spoke to her . . . what more would you have? Irina danced *avec tous les meilleurs cavaliers*, they were introduced to me one after another. . . . I lost count of them. Would you believe it, they simply followed us about in crowds; in the mazurka everybody wanted to choose her. One foreign diplomatist, learning that she lived in Moscow, said to the Tsar: " *Sire, décidément c'est Moscou qui est le centre de votre Empire*," and another diplomatist added, " *C'est une vraie révolution, Sire* " . . . *révélation* or *révolution* . . . something of the sort. . . . Yes, yes . . . it was . . . I must say, it was something extraordinary.'

'And what about Irina Pavlovna?' asked Litvinov, whose hands and feet had turned cold while the prince was speaking. 'Did she enjoy herself? Did she seem pleased?'

'Of course she enjoyed herself. Pleased? I should think she was! Though you know what she is, there's no making her out. Everybody was saying to me last night: "How extraordinary! *jamais on ne dirait que mademoiselle votre fille est à son premier bal.*" Count Reisenbach, for instance . . . but I expect you know him——'

' No, I don't know him in the least and have never met him.'

' My wife's cousin——'

' I don't know him, I tell you.'

' A *Kammerherr*, very rich, lives in Petersburg—an influential man, manages everything in Livonia. Till now he hasn't taken any notice of us . . . but, as you know, I don't mind that. *J'ai l'humeur facile, comme vous savez.* Well, that's the man. He sat down beside Irina, talked to her for a quarter of an hour, not more, and said afterwards to my wife: " *Ma cousine*," he said, " *votre fille est une perle; c'est une perfection*; everybody congratulates me on such a niece." And afterwards I saw he went up to . . . a very great personage and spoke to him, glancing at Irina all the time . . . and so did the other——'

' And so Irina Pavlovna will not show herself all day?' Litvinov asked again.

' No, she has a bad headache. She asked to give you her greetings and to thank you for your bouquet, *qu'on a trouvé charmant*. She needs a rest. . . . My wife has gone to pay some calls . . . and I too. . . .'

The prince coughed and shuffled his feet, as though at a loss for something more to say. Litvinov picked up his hat, and saying that he did not wish to hinder him and would call later to ask after Irina's health, went home.

A few steps from the Osinins' house he saw an

elegant brougham that had stopped by a policeman's sentry-box. A footman in a smart livery bending down carelessly from the box was asking the policeman which was Prince Pavel Vassilyevitch Osinin's house. Litvinov peeped into the carriage: it was occupied by a seedy-looking middle-aged man with a hooked nose, a hard mouth, and an arrogant expression on his wrinkled face. He was wrapped in a sable fur coat and from all appearances was an important official.

IX

Litvinov did not keep his promise to call later; he reflected that it would be better to put off his visit till the following day. When he came into the drawing-room that he knew only too well he found there the two younger sisters, Victorinka and Cleopatrinka. He said good morning to them and asked if Irina Pavlovna was better and if he could see her.

'Irinochka has gone out with mamma,' answered Victorinka, who in spite of her lisp was quicker than her sister.

'How ... gone out?' Litvinov repeated, and something began trembling deep within his breast. 'Doesn't she—doesn't she give you lessons at this time?'

'Irinochka won't give us lessons any more,' Victorinka answered.

'Not any more,' Cleopatrinka repeated.

'And is your papa at home?' Litvinov asked.

'Papa isn't at home either,' Victorinka went on. 'And Irinochka is not well: she cried and cried all through the night.'

'She cried?'

'Yes, she did ... Yegorovna told me, and her eyes are red as red and swollen. ...'

Litvinov walked twice up and down the room, slightly shuddering as though with a cold, and returned to his lodging. He had the kind of sensation one has when looking down from a very high tower: everything inside him seemed to faint, and a slow, sickening giddiness came over him. Dull perplexity and thoughts running helter-skelter, vague terror and numbness of expectation, strange, almost savage curiosity, the choking bitterness of unshed tears in his throat, a forced empty smile on his lips, and meaningless entreaty addressed to no one. . . . Oh, how cruel and humiliatingly hideous it all was! 'Irina does not want to see me,' kept running through his mind, 'that's clear; but why? What could have happened at that unfortunate ball? And how could she have changed all at once? So suddenly. . . .' (People constantly see that death comes suddenly, but cannot get used to its suddenness and think it senseless.) 'Not to have sent me a message, not to have explained anything——'

'Grigory Mihailovitch,' a strained voice said right into his ear.

Litvinov roused himself and saw his servant with a note in his hand. He recognized Irina's handwriting. . . . Before he had unsealed the note he had a sense of impending disaster; and he raised his shoulders and lowered his head as though trying to avoid a blow.

At last he plucked up his courage and tore open the envelope. This is what was written on a small sheet of note-paper:

'Forgive me, Grigory Mihailovitch. All is over between us: I am moving to Petersburg. I am horribly unhappy, but it's all settled. Evidently, it's my fate . . . but no, I don't want to justify myself. My forebodings have come true. Forgive me, forget me: I am not worthy of you. Irina.

'Be generous: don't attempt to see me.'

Litvinov read those lines and slowly sank back on the sofa as though someone had pushed him in the breast. He dropped the note, picked it up, read it again, whispered 'To Petersburg,' and dropped it again—that was all. A kind of stillness came over him; he actually rearranged the cushion under his head. 'Men wounded to death don't toss about,' he thought, 'it went as suddenly as it came. . . . It's quite natural; I always expected it.' He was lying to himself: he had never expected anything of the sort. 'She wept? . . . Did she? . . . What about? She did not love me! But of course it's all understandable and consistent with her character. She, she is not worthy of me! . . . Indeed!' He smiled bitterly. 'She did not herself know what power she had, but having seen its effect at that ball she couldn't of course be content with a humble student. . . . It's all quite natural.'

But then he recalled her tender words, her smile, and her eyes, those unforgettable eyes that he would never see again—the eyes that seemed to melt and shine at meeting his; he recalled one rapid, timid, burning kiss—and he suddenly broke into sobs—convulsive, furious, bitter. He turned over and, choking with tears and struggling for breath, buried his burning face in the cushion and bit it with savage relish, as though longing to tear to pieces both himself and everything around him. . . .

Alas! the gentleman whom Litvinov had seen the day before in the brougham was no other than Princess Osinin's cousin, Count Reisenbach, a *Kammerherr* and a man of wealth. He noticed the impression produced by Irina on great personages and instantly saw what advantages could be drawn from it '*mit etwas Accuratesse.*' Being a man of energy and knowing how to find favour with people, the count immediately made his plan. He decided to act quickly, in Napoleonic fashion.

'I'll take that original girl into my house in Petersburg,' he reflected. 'I'll make her my heiress, damn it all ... well, perhaps not of all my property; I have no children and she is a niece of mine, and my wife feels lonely.... Anyway, it's so much to the good to have a pretty face in one's drawing-room. Yes, yes, that's it: *es ist eine Idee, es ist eine Idee!* '

The thing was to dazzle and overwhelm the parents. 'They haven't a penny,' the count continued his reflections as he drove to Dogs' Square in his brougham, 'so they're not likely to make difficulties. They haven't such fine feelings as all that.... And perhaps I'll offer them a sum of money, too. And she? she too will agree. Honey is sweet ... she had a taste of it yesterday. It's just a whim of mine, I admit; so they may as well take advantage of it—the fools. I'll tell them: that's how it is; decide. Or else I'll take some other girl; an orphan would suit me even better. Yes or no, twenty-four hours for reflection, *und damit Punctum.*'

With these words on his lips the count appeared before Prince Osinin whom he had warned of his visit the night before, at the ball. There is no need to say much about the consequences of that visit. The count was not mistaken in his calculations: the prince and princess certainly made no difficulties and accepted a sum of money; Irina, too, consented before the twenty-four hours were over. It was not easy for her to break with Litvinov; she loved him, and after sending him her note, she almost fell ill, wept continually, and grew thin and pale. . . . Nevertheless, a month later the princess took her to Petersburg and settled her at the count's, entrusting her to the care of his wife—a very kind woman with the brains of a chicken, and rather like a chicken in appearance.

Litvinov left the university and joined his father in the country. His wound healed, little by little. At first he had no news of Irina at all, and indeed he avoided all conversation about Petersburg and Petersburg society. Then gradually rumours began to spread about her—not bad, but strange rumours; she was much talked of. The name of the young Princess Osinin, surrounded by a special halo of brilliance, was mentioned more and more often even in provincial society. It was uttered with curiosity, respect, and envy, like the name of Countess Vorotynsky once upon a time. At last came the news of her marriage. But Litvinov paid scarcely any attention to that last piece of information: he was already engaged to Tatyana.

The reader will probably have understood by now what was in Litvinov's mind when he cried out ' Can it be she?' And so we will return to Baden and take up again our interrupted story.

X

Litvinov was very late in going to sleep and he did not sleep long: the sun had just risen when he got up. The summits of the dark hills that could be seen from his window showed misty purple against the clear sky. 'How fresh it must be there, under the trees,' he thought—and he dressed hastily, glanced absent-mindedly at the bouquet that had opened even more luxuriantly during the night, took his stick, and set out for the famous 'Rocks' beyond the Old Castle. The morning enfolded him in its strong and gentle embrace. It was a joy to him to breathe, to move; the health of youth played in every fibre of his body; the very ground he trod on seemed resilient under his light feet. With every step he took he felt more and more gay and light-hearted. He walked in the dewy shade along the coarse sand of the paths bordered with fir-trees; the tips of their branches showed the light green of the fresh growth. 'How jolly it is!' he kept saying to himself.

Suddenly familiar voices reached his ears: he looked before him and saw Voroshilov and Bambaev walking towards him. He positively shuddered; like a school-boy hiding from his master he rushed to one side and hid behind a bush. 'Good Lord, let my compatriots go past me!' he prayed. He felt ready to pay any price if only they did not see him.... And they actually did not see him: the Good Lord let his compatriots go past. Voroshilov in his complacent cadet voice was holding forth to Bambaev on the various 'phases' of Gothic architecture, and Bambaev merely grunted approvingly; it was obvious that Voroshilov had been treating him to those 'phases' for some time, and the good-natured enthusiast was beginning to get bored. Stretching his neck and biting his lip Litvinov listened for some minutes to their retreating footsteps; the throaty or the nasal modulations of Voroshilov's instructive speech could be heard for a long while, but at last all was still. With a sigh of relief Litvinov left his hiding-place and walked on.

He wandered among the hills for a good three hours. Sometimes he left the path and jumped from stone to stone, slipping occasionally on the smooth moss; sometimes he sat down on a piece of rock under a beech or an oak-tree and thought pleasant thoughts to the unceasing murmur of rivulets overgrown with bracken, the restful rustle of leaves, the ringing song of a solitary blackbird. Light, pleasant drowsiness stole upon him as though embracing him from behind, and he dropped asleep . . . but suddenly he smiled and looked round: the gold and green of the forest and the forest air beat down softly on his eyes, and he closed them again with a smile. At last he wanted his breakfast and set out for the Old Castle where one could get a glass of good milk and coffee for a few kreutzers. But he had no sooner settled at one of the white-painted tables on the terrace before the castle than he heard horses snorting, and there appeared three carriages bringing a large company of ladies and gentlemen. Litvinov knew at once that they were Russian although they were all talking French . . . because they were talking French.

The ladies' dresses were elaborately smart; the gentlemen wore brand-new frock-coats, close-fitting and with a waist-line—which is not quite usual at the present day—grey speckled trousers, and very glossy town hats. A low black cravat tightly clasped the neck of each gentleman, and there was something military in all their bearing. They really were military men: Litvinov had come upon a picnic of young generals, persons of the highest social standing and considerable influence. Their importance showed itself in everything: in their restrained liveliness, charmingly dignified smiles, deliberately absent-minded expression, languid shrug of the shoulders, in the way they swayed their bodies and bent their knees; it was felt in the very sound of their voices that seemed to be amiably and fastidiously thanking a crowd of subordinates. All those warriors were excellently washed, shaved, and scented through and through with the true aroma of nobility and the Guards—a mixture of the best cigar smoke and wonderful patchouli. All had truly gentlemanly hands, white, large, with nails as hard as ivory; all had glossy moustaches, sparkling teeth, and beautiful skin, rosy on their cheeks and bluish on their chins. Some of the young generals were playful, others thoughtful; but the stamp of the highest decorum marked every one of them. Each seemed to be deeply conscious of his own dignity and the importance of the part he was to play in the state; each had a manner that was both severe and free, with a slight tinge of that sprightliness, that *diable m'emporte* which is so natural while travelling abroad. After settling down noisily and luxuriously, the company called the waiters, who hastened to serve them.

Litvinov hurried over his glass of milk, paid his bill and, putting on his hat, made his way past the generals' picnic. . . .

'Grigory Mihailovitch,' said a woman's voice. 'You don't recognize me?'

He stopped in spite of himself. That voice . . . that voice had too often made his heart beat in the old days. He turned round and saw Irina.

She was sitting at a table, her arms crossed over the back of a chair that had been pushed back. Bending her head on one side and smiling, she was looking at him kindly, almost joyfully.

Litvinov knew her at once, though she had changed since he last saw her ten years before and was no longer a girl but a woman. Her slender figure had developed and blossomed out, the outline of the once narrow shoulders reminded one now of the goddesses painted on the ceilings of old Italian palaces. But the eyes were the same and it seemed to Litvinov that they looked at him just as they had done before, in that little house in Moscow.

'Irina Pavlovna . . .' he said irresolutely.

'You do recognize me? I am so glad! How very ——' She stopped and drew herself up, blushing slightly. 'This is a very pleasant meeting,' she went on in French. 'Let me introduce you to my husband. Valérien, Monsieur Litvinov, *un ami d'enfance*; Valerian Vladimirovitch Ratmirov, my husband.'

One of the young generals, perhaps the most elegant

of all, got up from his chair and saluted Litvinov with the utmost politeness. The others frowned slightly, or, to be more exact, momentarily withdrew into themselves as though protesting beforehand against any contact with an unknown civilian; the ladies thought fit to screw up their eyes and smile slightly and even to look perplexed.

'Have you—have you been long in Baden?' asked General Ratmirov, preening himself in a curiously un-Russian way and evidently not knowing what to say to his wife's friend of childhood.

'A few days,' Litvinov answered.

'And do you intend to stay long?' the general continued politely.

'I haven't yet made up my mind.'

'Ah! That is very pleasant . . . very.'

The general paused. Litvinov too was silent. Both held their hats in their hands and bending forward and smiling, gazed at each other's eyebrows.

'*Deux gendarmes un beau dimanche,*' sang a bleareyed general with a look of permanent irritation on his yellowish face, as though he could not forgive himself his own appearance; he sang out of tune, of course—we have never yet come across a Russian nobleman who didn't. He was the only one among his companions who was not like a rose.

'Why don't you sit down, Grigory Mihailovitch,' Irina remarked at last.

Litvínov obeyed and sat down.

'I say, Valérien, give me some fire,' said in English another general, also young but already stout, with eyes that seemed to be staring into space, and thick silky whiskers into which he slowly plunged his snow-white fingers. Ratmirov handed him a silver match-box.

' *Avez-vous des papiros?* ' asked one of the ladies slurring her *r* in Parisian fashion.

' *De vrais papelitos, Comtesse.* '

' *Deux gendarmes un beau dimanche,*' the blear-eyed general began again, with exasperation.

' You must certainly come and see us,' Irina was saying to Litvinov meanwhile. ' We are staying at the Hôtel de l'Europe. I am always at home between four and six. It is so long since we met.'

Litvinov glanced at Irina; she did not lower her eyes.

' Yes, very long, Irina Pavlovna. Since Moscow.'

' Since Moscow,' she repeated. ' Come and see me, we'll talk and recall the old days. And do you know, Grigory Mihailovitch, you haven't changed much.'

' Indeed? But you have changed, Irina Pavlovna.'

' I've grown older.'

' No. That wasn't what I meant——'

' *Irène?* ' a lady with a yellow hat on her yellow hair called questioningly, after some whispering and tittering with the gentleman next to her. ' *Irène?* '

' I've grown older,' Irina went on, not answering the lady, ' but I haven't changed. No, no, I haven't changed in anything.'

' *Deux gendarmes un beau dimanche!* ' was heard again. The irritable general remembered only the first line of the popular song.

' The sore spot is still there, your excellency,' the stout general with whiskers said loudly with a comical intonation, probably hinting at some amusing incident, familiar to all the *beau-monde*, and with a short wooden

77

SMOKE

laugh stared into space again. The rest of the
company laughed too.

'What a sad dog you are, Boris,' Ratmirov remarked
in English in an undertone. He pronounced even
the name 'Boris' as if it were English.

'*Irène?*' the lady in the yellow hat said for the third
time. Irina turned sharply round to her.

'*Eh bien, quoi? que me voulez-vous?*'

'*Je vous le dirai plus tard,*' the lady answered coyly.
She was extremely unattractive, but full of airs and
graces; some wit said of her that she '*minaudait dans le
vide*'—coquetted in the void.

Irina frowned and impatiently shrugged her
shoulder.

'*Mais que fait donc Monsieur Verdier? Pourquoi ne
vient-il pas?*' a lady exclaimed, drawling out her words
in the way that is peculiar to the Russian pronunciation
and so unendurable to French ears.

'*Ah wooi, ah wooi, M'sieur Verdier, M'sieur Verdier,*'
moaned another, who might have come straight from
Arzamas.

'*Tranquillisez-vous, mesdames,*' Ratmirov intervened.
'*Monsieur Verdier m'a promis de venir se mettre à vos
pieds.*'

'He-he-he!' The ladies played with their fans.
The waiter brought several glasses of beer.

'*Bayerisch-Bier?*' asked the general with the whiskers, speaking in a bass voice and pretending to be
surprised—'*Guten Morgen!*'

'Do you know if Count Pavel is still there?' one
young general asked another coldly and listlessly.

[1] A small town in Central Russia. (Translator's note.)

78

' Yes, he is,' the other answered in the same tone. ' *Mais c'est provisoire.* They say Serge is to take his place.'

' Hm ! ' the first said through his teeth.

' Ye-es,' said the second, also through his teeth.

' I can't understand,' remarked the general who had been attempting to sing, ' I can't understand what possessed Paul to justify himself and give explanations. Well, he was hard on the tradesman, *ill ui a fait rendre gorge*, but what of it? He might have had his own reasons.'

' He was afraid of . . . being shown up in the press,' somebody muttered.

The irritable general flared up.

' Well, that's the limit ! the press ! being shown up ! If I had my say, all that I'd allow to be printed in the newspapers would be prices of meat and corn and advertisements of fur coats and boots for sale.'

' And of the sales of the nobles' estates by auction,' Ratmirov added.

' Yes, perhaps, as things are now. . . . But what a subject for conversation at Baden, *au Vieux Château* ! '

' *Mais pas du tout! pas du tout!* ' lisped the lady in the yellow hat. ' *J'adore les questions politiques.* '

' *Madame a raison,* ' remarked another general with an extremely pleasant and as it were girlish face. ' Why should we avoid those questions . . . even at Baden? ' With these words he glanced politely at Litvinov with an indulgent smile. ' A decent man must not renounce his convictions anywhere or under any circumstances. Isn't that so? '

' Of course,' answered the irritable general, also

glancing at Litvinov and as it were indirectly blowing him up, ' but I see no need——'

' No, no,' the indulgent general interrupted him, with the same mildness. ' Your friend Valerian Vladimirovitch has just mentioned the sales of the nobles' estates. Well? Isn't that a fact? '

' And there's no sale for them now—nobody wants them ! ' the irascible general exclaimed.

' That may be . . . that may be. But that's all the more reason why we should state that fact—that sad fact—at every opportunity. We are ruined—very well; we are humiliated—there's no denying it; but still we big landowners represent a certain principle . . . *un principe*. To defend that principle is our duty. *Pardon, madame*, I believe you dropped your handkerchief. When even the most exalted minds are, so to speak, clouded, we must humbly point '—the general pointed with his finger—' as citizens, to the abyss towards which everything is rushing. We must warn, we must say with respectful firmness: " Go back, go back. ". . . That's what we must say.'

' But we can't go back altogether, you know,' Ratmírov remarked thoughtfully.

The indulgent general merely smiled.

' Right back, right back, *mon très cher*. The further back the better.'

The general again politely glanced at Litvinov. The latter could not resist asking:

' Would you have us go back to the rule of the Seven Boyars,[1] your excellency?'

' Why not ! I am putting my opinion quite bluntly:

[1] In 1610, during the 'Time of Trouble.' (Translator's note.)

all that has been done must be—yes, must be undone.'

' Including the nineteenth of February? '[1]

' Yes—as far as possible. *On est patriote ou on ne l'est pas.* What about the emancipation? I shall be asked. Do you imagine the peasants enjoy their freedom? Ask them——'

' Just you try to take away that freedom ! ' Litvinov rejoined.

' *Comment nommez-vous ce monsieur?* ' the general whispered to Ratmirov.

' But what are you talking about? ' the stout general intervened; he evidently played the part of a spoiled child among his friends. ' About the press? About these scribblers? I'll tell you of an encounter I had with a scribbler—it was delightful ! I was told that a certain *folliculaire* had written a scurrilous article about me. Well, of course, I had him snapped up at once. They brought the man to me. "How is it, my dear *folliculaire*, that you go in for libel?" I asked him. "Has your patriotism got the better of you?" "It has," says he. " And do you like money, *folliculaire*?" says I. "I do," says he. Then, my dear sirs, I gave him the knob of my cane to sniff. " And do you like this, my angel? " " No," says he, " I don't like it." "Have a good sniff at it," says I, "my hands are clean." " I don't like it," was all he would say. " And I like it very much, my dear, though not for myself. Do you understand this allegory, my treasure?" "I do," says he. " Well, mind you be a good boy for the future. And now here's a fine silver rouble

[1] The emancipation of the serfs, 19th February 1861.
(Translator's note.)

for you.   Go, and bless me night and day." And
the scribbler went off.'

The general laughed, and again all laughed with him
—all except Irina, who did not even smile, but looked
rather gloomily at the speaker.

The indulgent general patted Boris on the shoulder.
' You 've invented it all on the spot, my dear friend.
. . . As though you would threaten anybody with a
cane. . . . Why, you haven't got one. *C'est pour faire
rire ces dames*—just for effect. But that's not the
point.   I said just now that we must go right back.   I
want to make myself clear.   I am not an enemy of
so-called progress; but all those universities and
seminaries and elementary schools, those students,
sons of the clergy, men of no class, all that rabble,
tout ce fond du sac, la petite propriété, pire que le prolétariat '
(the general uttered these words in a languid, almost
fainting voice) *'voilà ce qui m'effraie* . . . that's where
one must stop . . . and draw the line.' (He again
looked kindly at Litvinov.) ' Yes, we must draw
the line.   Bear in mind, no one in Russia asks for
anything, makes any demands. Self-government,
for instance, does any one ask for it? Do *you* ask
for it? Or you? Or you? Or you, *mesdames*?
You rule not only over yourselves, but over all of
us as it is.' (The general's handsome face was en-
livened by an amused smile.) 'My dear friends,
then why go cap in hand? Democracy is glad to
welcome you, it flatters you, it is ready to serve your
ends, but it's a double-edged weapon. Much better
have things done in the old, well-tried way . . . it's
much safer. Don't allow the mob to get presump-

tuous—but trust to the aristocracy which alone is strong. . . . That really would be better. And as to progress . . . I really have nothing against it. Only don't give us all those lawyers and juries and elected rural officials—and above all, don't interfere with discipline—as for the rest, you may build bridges and wharfs and hospitals, and there's no harm in lighting the streets with gas.'

' They've set fire to Petersburg from every quarter, there's progress for you !' the irascible general hissed.

' Why, you are bitter, I see,' the stout general observed, swaying lazily in his chair. ' You ought to be made a chief prosecutor; but in my opinion, *avec " Orphée aux enfers " le progrès a dit son dernier mot.'*

' *Vous dites toujours des bêtises,'* the lady from Arzamas tittered.

The general drew himself up.

' *Je ne suis jamais plus sérieux, madame, que quand je dis des bêtises.'*

' Monsieur Verdier has used this very phrase several times already,' Irina remarked in an undertone.

' *De la poigne et des formes!* ' the stout general exclaimed, ' *de la poigne surtout.* And that can be translated into Russian: " Be polite, but use your fists."'

' Ah, you naughty boy, you are incorrigible ! ' the indulgent general chimed in. ' *Mesdames,* don't listen to him, please. He wouldn't hurt a fly. He is content with devouring hearts.'

' No, Boris, that won't do,' Ratmirov began, after exchanging a look with his wife, ' joking is all very well, but that's going too far. Progress is an expression of the national life, that's what you mustn't forget. It's a symptom. One has to watch it.'

'Yes, of course,' the stout general replied, wrinkling his nose, 'we all know your ambition is to be a statesman!'

'Not at all. . . . Statesman, indeed! But one can't shut one's eyes to truth.'

'Boris' again thrust his fingers into his whiskers and stared into vacancy.

'National life is a very important matter, for in the development of a people, in the destinies, so to speak, of the fatherland——'

'*Valérien*,' Boris interrupted impressively, '*il y a des dames ici*. I didn't expect this of you. Are you trying to get on to a committee?'

'Thank heaven, they are all closed by now,' the irascible general broke in, and again began singing '*Deux gendarmes un beau dimanche* . . .'

Ratmirov raised a cambric handkerchief to his nose and gracefully subsided into silence; the indulgent general repeated 'Naughty boy! Naughty boy!' And Boris turned to the lady who coquetted in the void and, without lowering his voice or even changing his expression, began asking when she would 'reward his devotion,' for he was desperately in love with her and suffered beyond endurance.

During that conversation Litvinov felt more and more uncomfortable every moment. His pride—his honest plebeian pride—was roused. What had he, the son of a petty official, in common with those Petersburg military aristocrats? He loved all that they hated, he hated all that they loved—he saw it only too

84

clearly, he felt it with all his being. He thought their
jokes flat, their tone unendurable, their movements
affected; the very softness of their speech suggested
to him revolting contemptuousness—and yet he
seemed to feel timid in their presence, in the presence
of those men who were his enemies. . . . 'Ugh, how
disgusting! They are ill at ease in my presence, I
seem ridiculous to them,' he kept thinking, 'then why
do I stay? I must go—must go this minute.' Irina's
presence was not likely to detain him: she too roused
in him sensations that were none too happy. He got
up from his chair and began saying good-bye.

' Going already? ' Irina said, but on second thoughts
she did not detain him; she merely made him promise
that he would come to see her. General Ratmirov
bowed to him with the same refined courtesy, shook
hands, and walked with him to the end of the terrace.
But no sooner had Litvinov turned round the corner
than a general outburst of laughter reached his ears.
They were laughing not at him, but at the long-
expected Monsieur Verdier, who suddenly appeared
on the terrace in a Tyrolese hat and a blue smock,
riding a donkey; but Litvinov's cheeks grew hot and
he felt bitter; it was as though his tightly compressed
lips had been drawn together by wormwood.

' Contemptible, vulgar people! ' he muttered, forgetting that the few minutes he had spent in those
people's company had given him no reason for
judging them so harshly. And this was the world
which Irina, once his own Irina, had entered! She
moved in it, she lived in it, she was the queen of it;
she had sacrificed to it her own dignity, the best

feelings of her heart. . . . It evidently was as it should be; she evidently deserved no better fate! How glad he was that she had not thought of questioning him about his plans! He would have had to speak before 'them,' in 'their' presence. 'Never! not on any account!' Litvinov whispered, taking in deep breaths of the fresh air and almost running down the road to Baden. He was thinking of his betrothed, of his dear, good, holy Tatyana—and how pure, noble, and truthful she appeared to him! With what genuine tenderness he recalled her features, her words, her habits . . . how impatiently he looked forward to her return!

The quick walk calmed his nerves. Returning home he sat down at the table, took up a book and suddenly dropped it with a start. . . . What had happened to him? Nothing had happened, but Irina . . . Irina . . . all of a sudden his meeting her seemed to him marvellous, strange, incredible. Was it possible? He had met, he had spoken to that same Irina . . . and why was she free from that hateful stamp of worldliness which marked all the others so sharply? Why did he fancy that she seemed bored, or sad, or dissatisfied with her surroundings? She was in their camp, but she was not an enemy. And what could have made her turn to him in such a friendly way and ask him to come and see her?

Litvinov roused himself. 'Oh, Tanya, Tanya!' he exclaimed fervently, 'you alone are my angel, my good genius—you only do I love and will love all my life! I won't go to *her*. Let her be! Let her amuse herself with her generals!'

Litvinov took up his book once more.

XI

LITVINOV took up his book, but he did not feel like reading. He went for a little walk, listened to the music, had a look at the gambling, came back to his room and again tried to read—but it was no use. The time dragged by with curious dreariness. Pishchalkin, the well-meaning arbitrator of the peace, called and stayed for a good three hours. He talked, reasoned, asked questions, argued about exalted and about practical subjects, and at last poor Litvinov nearly howled with boredom. In the art of reducing people to a cold, miserable, desperate, and hopeless state of dullness Pishchalkin had no rivals—not even among men of the highest morals who are past masters at it. The very sight of his head with its smooth, closely cropped hair, of his dull, colourless eyes and his respectable nose made one feel melancholy, and his slow, sleepy-sounding baritone seemed to have been created for the purpose of enunciating clearly and with conviction such truths as that twice two is four and not five or three; that water is wet and virtue commendable, that private persons as well as the State, and the State as as well as private persons, need credit for financial operations. And in spite of all that he was an excellent man! But such is the fate with us in Russia: our excellent men are boring.

Pishchalkin withdrew. Then came Bindasov who

87

immediately and with great insolence requested
Litvinov to lend him a hundred guldens—and Litvinov
complied, although he was not interested in Bindasov
and indeed despised him, and knew for a fact that he
would never see his money again; besides, he needed
it himself. Why then did he lend it? the reader will
ask. The devil only knows! Russians are great at
that sort of thing. Let the reader recall, with his
hand on his heart, the number of times he too has
done things for no reason whatever. And Bindasov
did not even thank Litvinov: he asked for a glass of
Affenthaler (the Baden red wine), and without wiping
his lips walked out of the room, impudently stamping
with his boots. Litvinov was bitterly annoyed with
himself as he looked at the thick red nape of the
retreating bully.

By the afternoon post he received a letter from
Tatyana saying that her aunt was unwell and they
would not be able to come to Baden for another five
or six days. Litvinov was vexed by the news; it
increased his annoyance and he went to bed early in
a bad mood.

The day that followed was almost worse than the
preceding one. In the morning Litvinov's room was
crowded by his compatriots: Bambaev, Voroshilov,
Pishchalkin, the two officers, and the two Heidelberg
students all came together and stayed till dinner-time,
though they had soon exhausted their subjects of
conversation and were obviously bored. They did
not know what to do with themselves and having
come to Litvinov's lodgings, ' stuck ' there. At first
they spoke of Gubaryov's return to Heidelberg and

said that they ought to go and see him there; then they philosophized a little, discussed politics and touched on the Polish question; then they talked of gambling and *cocottes* and told scandalous anecdotes; at last they began telling stories about gluttons and men of exceptional strength. They trotted out the well-worn stories about the deacon who for a bet ate thirty-three salt herrings, the colonel of the Uhlans, Izyedinov, famous for his stoutness, the soldier who could break a beef bone against his own forehead, and other tales that were obvious inventions. Pish-chalkin himself related with a yawn that he knew a peasant woman in the Ukraine who weighed at her death over half a ton, and a landowner who could eat at luncheon three geese and a sturgeon. Bambaev suddenly grew enthusiastic and declared that he him-self could eat a whole sheep at one go, ' with condi-ments, of course.' Voroshilov blurted out something so absurd about a schoolfellow, an athletic cadet, that all were reduced to silence and after a pause looked at each other, picked up their hats, and went home.

Left alone, Litvinov tried to work, but his head seemed to have been filled with fumes, and he could not do anything that was worth while—and so the evening too was wasted. The following morning just as he was going out to have lunch someone knocked at his door. ' Good heavens, one of my yesterday's visitors again ! ' Litvinov thought and said ' *Herein !* ' with some trepidation.

The door opened quietly and Potugin walked in. Litvinov was greatly pleased to see him.

' Now this is really kind of you ! ' he said, warmly

pressing his unexpected visitor's hand. 'How very nice! I would certainly have called on you myself but you wouldn't tell me where you live. Please take a seat and put down your hat. Do sit down!'

Potugin stood in the middle of the room, shifting from one foot to the other, and, without answering Litvinov's friendly words, merely smiled and shook his head. He was obviously touched by Litvinov's warm welcome, but he looked slightly embarrassed.

'I am afraid there's a little misunderstanding . . .' he began with some hesitation. 'Of course, I am always very pleased . . . but to be exact . . . I've been sent to you.'

'You mean to say,' Litvinov said in a plaintive voice, 'that you wouldn't have come of your own accord?'

'Oh, no, not at all! But I . . . perhaps I wouldn't have ventured to trouble you to-day if I hadn't been asked to call on you. In short, I have a message for you.'

'From whom, may I ask?'

'From somebody you know—Irina Pavlovna Ratmirov. The day before yesterday you promised to call on her and you haven't been.'

Litvinov stared at Potugin with surprise.

'You know Madame Ratmirov?'

'As you see.'

'Do you know her well?'

'I am a friend of hers in a sense.'

Litvinov was silent.

'Allow me to ask,' he began at last, 'do you know why Irina Pavlovna wants to see me?'

Potugin walked up to the window.

' I do, in a way. So far as I can tell she is very glad to have met you and wants to renew your former relations.'

' Renew . . . ' Litvinov repeated. ' Excuse my inquisitiveness, but may I ask you another question? Do you know what our relations were? '

' No—not really. But I believe,' Potugin added, turning suddenly towards Litvinov and looking at him with friendly eyes, ' I believe they must have been good. Irina Pavlovna spoke very highly of you and I had to promise her I would bring you. Will you come? '

' When? '

' Now—at once.'

Litvinov threw up his hands in surprise.

' Irina Pavlovna,' Potugin went on, ' thinks that the—how shall I put it?—the surroundings in which you met her the day before yesterday could not have impressed you very favourably; but she wants me to tell you that the devil is not so black as he is painted.'

' Hm. . . . Does the saying specially apply to those . . . surroundings? '

' Yes . . . and in general.'

' Hm. . . . Well, and what do you yourself, Sozont Ivanitch, think about the devil? '

' I think, Grigory Mihailitch, that at any rate he is not what he is painted.'

' Is he better? '

' It's hard to say whether he is better or worse, but he is different. Well, shall we go? '

' But do sit down for a bit to begin with. To tell you the truth it still seems rather strange to me——'

'What, may I ask?'

'How could you, of all people, have come to be a friend of Irina Pavlovna's?'

Potugin glanced at himself.

'Considering my appearance and my social position it certainly does seem improbable; but you know, Shakespeare himself has said, "There are more things in heaven and earth, Horatio," and so on. Life is no joke. Here's a comparison for you: there's a tree before you, and there is no wind; how is a leaf on a lower branch to touch a leaf on the top one? It can't be done. But a storm blows up, everything is thrown into confusion—and the two leaves touch.'

'Aha! So there have been storms?'

'Of course! There's no escaping them. But no more arguing, it's time we were going.'

Litvinov still hesitated.

'Good heavens!' Potugin said with a comical grimace. 'What's come over young men nowadays! A most charming lady invites them, sends special messengers for them, and they make difficulties! Shame on you, my dear sir, shame on you! Here's your hat. Take it, and *vorwärts!* as our friends, the ardent Germans, say.'

Litvinov still hesitated, but he ended by taking his hat and leaving the room together with Potugin.

XII

THEY arrived at one of the best hotels in Baden and asked for Madame Ratmirov. The hall porter inquired what their names were and said at once, ' *Die Frau Fürstin ist zu Hause.*' He took them upstairs, knocked at the door, and announced them. ' *Die Frau Fürstin* ' received them immediately; she was alone: her husband had gone to Carlsruhe to meet an influential official personage who was travelling through that town.

When Potugin and Litvinov entered the room, Irina was sitting at a small table doing embroidery. She quickly flung her work aside, pushed away the table, and stood up; a look of genuine pleasure came into her face. She was wearing a morning dress with a high collar; the beautiful lines of her arms and shoulders showed through the light material; her hair, carelessly twisted into a knot, came low over her delicate neck.

Irina gave a quick glance to Potugin, murmured ' *Merci,*' and holding out her hand to Litvinov, reproached him amiably for his forgetfulness. ' And an old friend, too! ' she added.

Litvinov tried to apologize. ' *C'est bien, c'est bien,*' she said hurriedly, and in a friendly way taking his hat from him, as it were by force, made him sit down. Potugin sat down also, but got up again at once, and saying that he had urgent business and

93

would call again after dinner, took his leave. Irina gave him another quick look and a friendly nod, but did not detain him. As soon as he disappeared behind the curtained door, she turned to Litvinov with impatient eagerness.

'Grigory Mihailitch,' she said in Russian in her soft ringing voice, ' we are alone at last and I can tell you that I am very glad we have met, for it gives me a chance' (Irina looked him straight in the face) 'to ask your forgiveness.'

Litvinov gave an involuntary start. He had not expected such a sudden attack. He had not expected that she would be the first to speak of the old times.

'Forgiveness—for what?' he muttered.

Irina flushed.

'For what? you know for what,' she brought out, turning slightly away. 'I wronged you, Grigory Mihailitch . . . though of course it was my fate' (Litvinov recalled her letter) 'and I do not repent . . . it would be too late to do that, in any case. But when I met you so suddenly I said to myself that we must at all costs be friends—and it would hurt me very much if that couldn't be—and it seems to me that the first thing to do is to have it out with you, at once and once for all, so that afterwards there should not be any . . . *gêne,* any awkwardness, once for all, Grigory Mihailitch, and you must tell me that you forgive me, or else I'll suspect that you harbour . . . *de la rancune. Voilà!* It may be a great presumption on my part, for probably you have forgotten everything ages ago, but in any case, tell me that you've forgiven me.'

94

Irina said all this without stopping to take breath and Litvinov noticed that tears—yes, tears—glistened in her eyes.

'Why, Irina Pavlovna,' he began hastily, 'for shame! the idea of your apologizing and asking my forgiveness! What happened is past and gone, and I can only wonder that amidst the brilliance that surrounds you, you still remember the humble companion of your early youth.'

'It surprises you?' Irina said softly.

'It touches me,' Litvinov went on, 'for I could never have believed——'

'But all the same you haven't told me that you forgive me,' Irina interrupted him.

'I am sincerely glad of your happiness, Irina Pavlovna, and wish you with all my heart all that is best on earth. . . .'

'And you don't remember evil?'

'I remember only the beautiful moments for which I was once indebted to you.'

Irina held out both her hands to him. Litvinov clasped them warmly and did not let them go at once. Something long forgotten secretly stirred in his heart at that soft touch. Irina was again looking him straight in the face, but this time she was smiling. And for the first time he too looked straight and attentively at her. . . . He recognized once more the features so dear to him in the past, the fathomless eyes with their wonderful eyelashes, the mole on her cheek, the special way her hair lay over her forehead, the habit of slightly twitching her eyebrows and twisting her lips in a particularly delightful and amusing way—he recognized it all. . . . But how beautiful she had grown! What feminine charm, what vigour there was in her young body! and no rouge, no paint, no powder, nothing false on the fresh, clear face. . . . Yes, she was indeed a beauty.

Litvinov's mind wandered. . . . He was still looking at her, but his thoughts were far away. Irina noticed this.

'Well, that's splendid,' she said aloud, 'now my conscience is at rest and I can satisfy my curiosity.'

'Curiosity?' Litvinov repeated as though not quite understanding her.

'Yes, yes—I am determined to know what you have been doing all this time, what your plans are; I want to know everything, everything—how, what, when. . . . And you must tell me the truth, for I warn you, I have not lost sight of you—so far as it was possible. . . .'

'Haven't lost sight of me, you — there — in Petersburg?'

' "Amidst the brilliance that surrounded me," as you put it just now. No, I didn't lose sight of you. We'll talk about that brilliance another time, and now you must tell me your story. Make it long, don't hurry over it, no one will disturb us. Ah, how lovely that will be!' Irina added, settling down in her arm-chair and gaily preening herself. 'Well, start away!'

'Before beginning, I must thank you,' Litvinov said.

'What for?'

'For the flowers I found in my room.'

'What flowers? I know nothing about it.'

'How is that?'

'I tell you I know nothing. . . . But I am waiting—waiting for your story. What a dear that Potugin is, to have brought you!'

Litvinov pricked up his ears.

'Have you known this Mr. Potugin long?'

'Yes . . . but do begin your story.'

'And do you know him well?'

'Oh, yes!' Irina sighed. 'There were special reasons. . . . You've heard, of course, about Elise Belsky . . . the one who died such an awful death? Oh, I've forgotten that you don't know the scandals of our set—what a blessing you don't! Oh, *quelle chance!* to have at last, at last met someone who is real and knows nothing about us! And one can talk Russian to him, even if it be bad Russian, and not that everlasting, horrid, colourless Petersburg French!'

'And, you say, Potugin was connected with——'

'It hurts me to speak of it,' Irina interrupted him. 'Elise was my best friend at school, and afterwards, in Petersburg, we saw each other continually. She confided all her secrets to me: she was very unhappy and suffered a great deal. Potugin behaved beautifully, with real chivalry, in all that affair. He sacrificed himself. It was only then that I recognized his true worth. But we've wandered off the point. I am waiting for you to tell me about yourself, Grigory Mihailitch.'

'But my story can't be of the slightest interest to you, Irina Pavlovna.'

'That's no business of yours, you know.'

' Just think, we haven't seen each other for ten years, ten whole years. Much water has flowed by since then.'

' Not water only! Not water only! ' she repeated with a peculiar, bitter expression. ' That's why I want to hear about you.'

' And besides, I really don't know where to begin.'

' At the beginning. From the time that you . . . that I moved to Petersburg. You left Moscow then. Do you know, I have never been back to Moscow since.'

' Really?'

' At first it was impossible, and afterwards when I was married——'

' Have you been married long?'

' Four years.'

' Have you any children? '

' No,' she answered dryly.

Litvinov paused.

' And before your marriage, did you live all the time at that—what's his name—Count Reisenbach's? '

Irina looked at him attentively as though to make sure why he was asking the question.

' No,' she said at last.

' So then your parents—— By the way, I never asked after them. Are they——? '

' They are both well.'

' And living in Moscow as before? '

' Yes, in Moscow as before.'

' And your brothers and sisters? '

' They are all right, I've provided for all of them.'

' Ah! ' Litvinov glanced at Irina from under his

eyebrows. 'It's really you, Irina Pavlovna, and not I, who should do the telling, if only——'

He suddenly pulled himself up.

Irina raised her hands to her face and twisted her wedding-ring on her finger.

'Well, I don't say no,' she said at last, 'some time ... perhaps. ... But you must speak first ... because, you see, though I did keep watch on you, I know next to nothing about you, while you ... you must have heard quite enough about me. Isn't that so? You have heard about me, haven't you?'

'You occupied too prominent a place in society not to be talked about ... especially in the provinces, where I was, and where they believe every rumour.'

'And did you believe those rumours? And what sort of rumours were they?'

'To tell you the truth, Irina Pavlovna, they reached me very seldom. I led a very secluded life.'

'How was that? Why, you were in the militia in the Crimea?'

'You know that too?'

'As you see. I tell you, you've been watched.'

Litvinov was astonished again.

'But then why must I tell you what you know already?' he said in an undertone.

'Why? Just to do what I ask you. You see, I am asking it of you, Grigory Mihailovitch.'

Litvinov inclined his head and began, somewhat confusedly, to tell Irina the main facts of his uneventful past. He often paused and looked at her questioningly as though to ask whether she had had enough. But she insisted on his going on; pushing her hair behind her ears and leaning on the arm of the chair she seemed to take in every word of his with strained attention. And yet an onlooker watching her expression might have imagined that she did not listen to Litvinov at all, but was simply lost in contemplation. . . . And it was not Litvinov she was contemplating, though he blushed with confusion under her persistent gaze. Another life was arising before her —not his, but her own life.

Litvinov did not finish his story but broke off from a growing unpleasant sense of awkwardness. This time Irina said nothing to him and did not ask him to go on. She pressed the palm of her hand to her eyes as though she were tired, and slowly leaning back in her arm-chair remained motionless. Litvinov waited a little and, reflecting that his visit had lasted more than two hours, was about to pick up his hat when suddenly the rapid creak of fine patent boots was heard in the next room, and Valerian Vladimirovitch Ratmirov, preceded by that same aristocratic perfume, walked into the room.

Litvinov got up from his chair and exchanged bows with the good-looking general. Irina slowly took away her hand from her face and looking coldly at her husband said in French: ' Oh, you are back already ! But what time can it be? '

' It is close on four o'clock, *chère amie*, and you are not dressed yet—the princess will be expecting us,' answered the general, and elegantly bending his slim waist in Litvinov's direction added with the languid playfulness peculiar to him: ' Evidently your amiable guest made you forget the time.'

SMOKE

The reader will allow us at this point to tell him a few things about General Ratmirov. His father was the natural son of a grandee of Alexander I's reign and a pretty French actress. The grandee secured his son's social position but left him no money—and that son (the father of our general) had not succeeded in amassing a fortune; when he died he had the rank of a colonel in the police. A year before his death he had married a handsome young widow who had had to seek his protection. Their son, Valerian Vladimirovitch, was admitted, through influence, to the *Corps des Pages* and soon attracted his superiors' attention—not so much by his success in studies as by his military bearing, excellent manners, and good behaviour (though he did not escape punishments inevitably inflicted in the old days on all the pupils of military schools). He got a commission in the Guards and made a brilliant career thanks to his modest cheerfulness, skill in dancing, splendid riding as an orderly on parades (using other people's horses for the most part), and chiefly to a special art of treating his superiors with respectful familiarity and a kind of subdued and gentle fawning tinged with the lightest possible shade of liberalism. That liberalism had not prevented him, however, from flogging fifty peasants in a village in White Russia where he had been sent to put down a riot. He had an attractive and extremely youthful appearance; rosy-cheeked, smooth, slender, and clinging, he enjoyed wonderful success with women: aristocratic old ladies were simply mad on him. Careful from habit, silent by calculation, General Ratmirov moved in the highest circles, like an industrious bee collecting honey even from the poorest flowers. Without any moral sense, without any knowledge, but with the reputation of a man of business, a flair for people, and a grasp of circumstances, and above all, with an unshakable determination to seek his own good—he had at last every prospect open to him.

Litvinov smiled with constraint, and Irina merely shrugged her shoulders.

'Well,' she said in the same cold voice, 'did you see the count?'

'Oh, yes. He sends you his greetings.'

'Ah! Is he as stupid as ever, that patron of yours?'

Ratmirov did not answer, but gave a slight nasal laugh as though to express his condescension to a woman's erratic judgment. Kindly disposed grown-up people respond with the same kind of laughter to children's foolish pranks.

'Yes,' Irina added, 'your count's stupidity is really striking, and heaven knows I've seen enough in that line.'

'You sent me to him yourself,' the general remarked through his teeth, and turning to Litvinov asked him whether he was drinking the Baden waters.

'But I am perfectly well, I am thankful to say,' Litvinov answered.

'That's the best thing of all,' the general continued with an amiable smile, 'and, generally speaking, people come to Baden not for medical purposes; but the waters here are very effectual, *je veux dire*, *efficaces*, and those who, like myself, suffer from a nervous cough——'

Irina stood up suddenly. 'We'll meet again, Grigory Mihailovitch, and I hope soon,' she said in French, interrupting her husband contemptuously, 'but now I must go and dress. That old princess is unendurable with her everlasting *parties de plaisir* that bore one stiff.'

'You are very hard on every one to-day,' her husband remarked as he slipped away into the next room.

Litvinov walked to the door. Irina stopped him.

'You've told me everything,' she said, 'but you concealed the chief thing. . . .'

'What is that?'

'I hear you are engaged to be married?'

Litvinov flushed crimson. It was true that he intentionally avoided mentioning Tanya, but he was fearfully annoyed, first at Irina's knowing about his engagement, and secondly at her catching him out, as it were, in his desire to conceal it from her. He was completely at a loss; Irina did not take her eyes off him.

'Yes, I am,' he said at last and walked out.

Ratmirov came back into the room.

'Well, why don't you dress?' he asked.

'You must go alone; I have a headache.'

'But the princess——'

Irina measured her husband with her glance from head to foot, turned her back on him, and went to her boudoir.

XIII

LITVINOV was greatly displeased with himself; it was as though he had lost at roulette or failed to keep a promise. An inner voice told him that as Tanya's betrothed, as a man who has reached the years of discretion, no longer a boy, he ought not to have yielded to the promptings of curiosity or the seductions of remembrance. ' Much need there was to go!' he argued with himself. 'It's nothing but coquetry on her part, just a whim, a caprice. . . . She is bored, she is tired of everything and so she snatched at me . . . a gourmand fancies sometimes a piece of black bread. . . . Well, that's all very fine. But why on earth did I go? As though I could feel anything but—contempt for her!' He uttered those last words even mentally with a certain effort. ' Of course there's no danger whatever and there cannot be,' he went on reflecting. 'I know with whom I have to deal. But still, one shouldn't play with fire— I won't set foot in her house again.'

Litvinov did not dare, or could not as yet, confess to himself how beautiful Irina appeared to him and how much she attracted him.

The day again passed slowly and drearily. At dinner Litvinov happened to sit next to an imposing-looking *bel homme* with a waxed moustache, who sat in silence, puffing and staring about him, but, hiccuping suddenly, proved to be a fellow country-man, for he at once remarked angrily in Russian, 'I said I ought not to have had that melon!'

In the evening, too, nothing pleasant happened. Bindasov won at the roulette in Litvinov's presence four times as much as he had borrowed from him, but instead of returning his debt he looked Litvinov menacingly in the face, as though intending to punish him all the more for having been a witness of his winnings. The following morning a crowd of his compatriots descended upon Litvinov again; having got rid of them with some difficulty he set off to the hills, and ran into Irina—he pretended not to recognize her and walked quickly past. Then he met Potugin and spoke to him, but Potugin answered reluctantly. He was leading by the hand a smartly dressed little girl with fair, almost white fluffy hair, large dark eyes in a pale, sickly-looking little face and the peremptory and impatient expression peculiar to spoiled children.

Litvinov spent two hours on the hills and was returning home by the Lichtenthal Avenue. A lady, sitting on a bench, with a blue veil over her face, got up quickly and walked up to him. He recognized Irina.

'Why do you avoid me, Grigory Mihailovitch?' she said in the unsteady voice that betokens long-suppressed emotion.

Litvinov was taken aback.

'I avoid you, Irina Pavlovna?'

'Yes, yes—you. . . .'

Irina seemed agitated, almost angry.

'You are mistaken, I assure you.'

' No, I am not. Do you suppose I didn't see this morning—when we met—that you recognized me? Didn't you? Tell me! '

' I really—Irina Pavlovna——'

' Grigory Mihailovitch, you are a straightforward man, you always speak the truth: tell me, you did recognize me, didn't you? You turned away on purpose? '

Litvinov glanced at Irina. Her eyes shone with a strange brilliance, and her cheeks and lips showed deadly white through the thick mesh of the veil. There was something irresistibly sorrowful and appealing in her expression, in the very sound of her broken whisper. Litvinov could pretend no longer.

' Yes—I did recognize you,' he brought out with some effort. Irina shuddered slightly, and slowly dropped her hands.

' Then why didn't you come up to me? ' she whispered.

' Why—why? ' Litvinov walked off the path and Irina followed him in silence. ' Why? ' he repeated again; his face suddenly felt hot, and bitter resentment gripped his heart and his throat. ' You—you ask that, after all that has passed between us? Not now, of course, not now, but there . . . there . . . in Moscow.'

' But we decided, you promised, you know——' Irina began.

' I've promised nothing. Excuse my speaking bluntly, but you ask for the truth. Judge for yourself: how can I explain your—I hardly know how to call it—your insistence, except by coquetry—which I confess I can't understand—by a desire to find out how much power you still have over me? Our paths have gone so far apart! I've forgotten the past, I've got over it long ago, I've become a different man; you are married, you are happy—at any rate in appearance—you have an enviable position in society—then why seek me out, what's the point of it? What am I to you, or you to me? We cannot even understand each other now, there is absolutely nothing in common between us, neither in the present nor in the past! Especially—especially in the past!'

Litvinov said all this hastily, jerkily, without turning his head. Irina stood still and only at times faintly raised her hands towards him. It was as though she implored him to stop and hear her, and at his last words she slightly bit her lower lip as if to suppress the pain of a sudden sting.

'Grigory Mihailitch,' she said at last in a calmer voice, walking still further away from the path where people passed occasionally. Litvinov in his turn followed her. 'Grigory Mihailitch, believe me: if I could imagine that I still had a grain of power over you I would be the first to avoid you. If I haven't done so, if I ventured, in spite of my . . . guilt in the past, to renew our acquaintance, it was because— because——'

'Because of what?' Litvinov asked almost rudely.

'Because,' Irina went on with sudden intensity, 'I felt too unbearably, too unendurably stifled in this "society," in this "enviable position" of which you speak; because when I met you, a real, live man after all those lifeless puppets—you saw specimens of them

107

the other day at the Vieux Château—I was glad as of a spring in the desert—and you call me a coquette, and suspect me, and repulse me on the pretext that I really did wrong you, and wronged myself still more.'

'You've chosen your lot yourself, Irina Pavlovna,' Litvinov brought out sullenly, still turning away from her.

'Yes, yes, I know . . . and I don't complain, I have no right to complain,' Irina said hastily; Litvinov's very harshness seemed to be a secret solace to her. 'I know you must blame me and I don't justify myself, I only want to explain my feeling to you, I want to convince you that I am in no mood for coquetry. . . . As though I could flirt with you! Why, there is no sense in it. . . . When I saw you, all that was good in me, all my youth, woke up in me—the time when I hadn't yet chosen my lot—all that lies there, in the streak of brightness behind those ten years——'

'Come, that's too much! So far as I know, the brightness in your life began precisely after we parted. . . .'

Irina raised her handkerchief to her lips.

'It's very cruel what you are saying, Grigory Mihailitch; but I cannot be angry with you. Oh, no, it wasn't brightness, it wasn't happiness I found after leaving Moscow. I haven't known one instant, one minute of happiness . . . believe me, whatever others may tell you. If I were happy, I couldn't talk to you as I am talking now. . . . I tell you again, you don't know what those people are like. . . . They understand nothing, they have no sympathy for anything, they haven't even intelligence, *ni esprit, ni intelligence*, only

savoir faire and cunning; at bottom, they don't care a
scrap either for music, or art, or poetry. You'll say
that I too was fairly indifferent to all that—but not to
such an extent, Grigory Mihailitch, not to such an
extent! It's not a society lady standing before you
now—you've got only to look to see that—not a
" lioness "—that's what they call us, I believe—but
a poor, poor creature who really deserves to be pitied.
Don't be surprised at my words—pride is nothing
to me now! I am holding out my hand to you like
a beggar, don't you understand? like a beggar. I
am begging for alms,' she added impulsively, unable
to control herself, ' I am begging for alms, and
you——'

Her voice failed her. Litvinov raised his head and
looked at her; she was breathing quickly and her lips
trembled. His heart beat fast and the feeling of
resentment disappeared.

' You say our paths have diverged,' Irina continued.
' I know you are marrying from inclination, you have
planned out your life, yes, all that is true, but we
haven't become strangers to each other, Grigory
Mihailitch, we can still understand each other. Or
do you imagine that I've grown quite dull, have
completely sunk into this quagmire? Oh, please
don't think that! Let me have some respite from it,
I beg you, if only for the sake of those past days, since
you refuse to forget them. Do so, that our meeting
may not have been in vain—that would be too
bitter; it won't last long in any case. . . . I do not
know how to speak properly, but you'll understand
me, for I ask little, very little . . . only a little sympathy,

only that you shouldn't repulse me, that you should give me a breathing space——'

Irina broke off, there were tears in her voice. She heaved a sigh and, glancing at Litvinov timidly with an entreating, sidelong look, held out her hand to him.

He slowly took it and pressed it faintly.

' Let's be friends,' Irina whispered.

' Friends,' Litvinov repeated dreamily.

' Yes, friends. . . . Or if that's too much to ask, let us at any rate be friendly. . . . Let us behave simply, as though nothing had ever happened.'

' As though nothing had happened,' Litvinov repeated again. ' You said just now that I refused to forget the old days . . . well, and what if I cannot forget them? '

A blissful smile flitted across Irina's face but disappeared at once, giving way to an anxious, almost frightened look.

' You must be like me, Grigory Mihailitch, and remember only the good; and above all, give me now your word—your word of honour——'

' To do what? '

' Not to avoid me . . . not to grieve me needlessly. Will you promise? Tell me ! '

' Yes.'

' And harbour no more bad thoughts? '

' No—but I still cannot understand you.'

' That's not necessary . . . though you'll understand me right enough, presently. But you promise? '

' I've already said yes.'

' Well, thank you. Now mind, I am used to trusting

you. I shall expect you to-day, to-morrow, I shall not go out. And now I must leave you. The duchess is coming along the avenue . . . she's seen me, and I must go up to her. Good-bye . . . give me your hand, *vite*, *vite!* Good-bye.'

Irina warmly pressed Litvinov's hand and went towards an imposing-looking middle-aged lady who was walking with a heavy step along the avenue accompanied by two other ladies and an extremely dignified liveried footman.

' *Eh bonjour, chère madame,*' said the lady, as Irina respectfully curtseyed before her. ' *Comment allez-vous aujourd'hui? Venez un peu avec moi.*'

' *Votre Altesse a trop de bonté,*' Irina's ingratiating voice was heard in reply.

XIV

LITVINOV waited till the duchess with her retinue had gone out of sight and also went down the avenue. He could not give himself a clear account of what he was feeling: he was ashamed and even alarmed, and yet his vanity was flattered. . . . The unexpected explanation with Irina had caught him unawares; her rapid, impulsive words had passed over him like a thunder-shower.

'Queer creatures those society women are,' he thought, 'so inconsistent . . . and how perverted they are by the environment in which they live and which they themselves feel to be hideous. . . .' In truth he was not thinking that at all, but was mechanically repeating those hackneyed phrases as though wishing to get rid of other, more anxious thoughts. He knew that he must not think seriously at the moment or else he would probably have to blame himself, and he walked on slowly, observing with an almost exaggerated attention everything he came across. . . . He suddenly found himself next a seat, saw somebody's feet in front of it, looked up from them; the feet belonged to a man who sat on the seat reading a newspaper; the man proved to be Potugin. Litvinov gave a slight exclamation. Potugin put down the newspaper and looked at Litvinov attentively, without a smile; Litvinov looked at Potugin, also attentively and also without a smile.

' May I sit beside you? ' he asked at last.

' Certainly, by all means. Only I warn you: if you wish to talk with me, you mustn't mind my being in a most misanthropic mood—everything appears to me in an exaggeratedly bad light.'

' That's all right, Sozont Ivanitch,' Litvinov replied, sitting down beside him. ' In fact it's very appropriate. . . . But what put you in that mood? '

' I oughtn't to feel cross, really,' Potugin began. ' I have just read in the paper about the proposed reforms of the law courts in Russia and I am deeply gratified to see that at last our leaders have thought better of it and refrained from tacking a home-grown tail on to the clear and obvious European logic under the pretext of originality or national feeling; on the contrary, they are taking a good thing in its entirety though it's foreign. It's bad enough to have given in about the peasant land—it will be no easy job to get rid of communal ownership! Certainly I ought not to be cross to-day, but as ill luck would have it I ran across a Russian " born genius " and had a talk with him—and these born geniuses and self-taught men will give me no peace when I'm in my grave.'

' What born genius? ' Litvinov asked.

' Oh, there's a man knocking about here who fancies himself a musical genius. " Of course," he says, " I am nothing, I am a cipher, because I haven't been trained, but I have incomparably more melodies and ideas in my head than Meyerbeer." To begin with, I say, " Why haven't you been trained? " and secondly, let alone Meyerbeer, the humblest German flute-player modestly piping his part in the humblest German orchestra has twenty times as many ideas as all our " born geniuses " put together. Only, the flutist keeps his ideas to himself and does not boast of them in the land of Mozarts and Haydns, while our un- tutored musician has no sooner produced a trumpery waltz or song than he begins to strut about with his hands in his pockets and a sneer on his lips—he's a genius! It's the same thing with painting and everything else. Oh, these natural geniuses! Why, everybody knows that people boast of them only where there's no real art, no real deeply rooted science. Surely it's time we did away with all this boasting, all this vulgar rubbish, together with the trite phrases that in Russia no one dies of hunger, that travelling by road is faster than anywhere, and that we are more than a match for any one? They keep bragging of the Russians' gifted nature, of their marvellous instinct, and of Kulibin. . . . But what sort of giftedness is that, my good sirs? It's like talking in one's sleep, like semi-animal cunning. Instinct! Fine thing to boast of! If you take an ant in the forest and carry it a mile away from its ant-heap, it will find its way home; a man can't do anything of the kind, but what of it? Is he inferior to an ant? Instinct, however marvellous, is not worthy of man: reason, simple, sound, ordinary reason is our true heritage and our pride. Reason plays no marvellous tricks— that's why everything rests upon it. And as for Kulibin, who without any knowledge of mechanics contrived to make some hideous clock—I should have that clock pilloried: see, good people, how *not* to make clocks ! Kulibin himself is not to blame, of course, but his case is hopeless. To praise Telushkin's courage and agility because he climbed on to the Admiralty spire is right enough—why not?—but it's absurd to shout that he put the German architect's nose out of joint, and say, What's the good of those Germans?—they do nothing but fleece us. . . . He didn't put any German's nose out of joint: a scaffolding had to be built round the spire after all, and it had to be repaired in the usual way. Don't, for heaven's sake, encourage the idea in Russia that anything can be achieved without learning ! No, you may be as clever as they make them, but you must study, study from the A B C ! Or else draw in your horns and be quiet. Ugh, it's made me quite hot ! '

Potugin took off his hat and fanned himself with his handkerchief.

' Russian painting,' he began again, ' Russian art ! I know Russian pretensions and Russian impotence, but I am sorry to say I haven't yet come across Russian painting. For twenty years we've worshipped that puffy nonentity Bryullov and imagined that we had a school of painting of our own and that, indeed, all others weren't a patch on it. . . . Russian art, ha-ha-ha ! ho-ho-ho ! '

' But wait a minute, Sozont Ivanitch,' Litvinov remarked. ' Don't you think anything of Glinka either? '

Potugin scratched himself behind his ear.

' Exceptions, as you know, merely prove the rule, but in this case too we couldn't avoid boasting ! No one would dispute that Glinka really was a remarkable musician who was prevented by circumstances, both inner and outer, from becoming the founder of the Russian opera; but no, that's not good enough! He must at once be promoted to a commander-in-chief, a lord marshal of music, and other nations must be put in their place: they, if you please, have nothing like it. And one is immediately told of some "mighty" home-grown genius whose works are merely a pitiful imitation of second-rate foreign composers— second-rate ones are the easiest to imitate. Nothing like it, indeed! Oh, poor silly barbarians, who don't understand what tradition in art means and who imagine that artists are something like the strong man Rappo: "A foreigner," they say, "can lift only thirteen stone with one hand, and our man lifts twenty-six!" Nothing like it!... And I'll tell you, if I may, something I keep recalling: this spring I went to the Crystal Palace near London; as you know it contains a kind of exhibition of all that human ingenuity has achieved—so to speak, an encyclopaedia of humanity. Well, I wandered among all those machines and implements and statues of great men, and thought to myself: Suppose an order were issued that if a nation disappeared off the face of the earth, all that it had invented was immediately to disappear from the Crystal Palace—our mother, Orthodox Russia, might sink into the nethermost pit, the dear creature, without disturbing a single nail or pin at the exhibition. Everything would remain in its place, for even the samovar, the bast shoes, and the knout—those famous articles of ours—were not invented by us. One could not make such an experiment even with the Sandwich

Islands: their inhabitants invented some kind of boats and spears, and visitors to the Palace would notice their absence. It's slander! It's too severe! you'll say, perhaps. And I shall say, first, that I'm no good at cooing while I am finding fault, and, secondly, that it's not only the devil, but even one's own self that people dare not look straight in the face, and that it's not only children who like being lulled to sleep. Our old inventions made their way to us from the East, and the new ones we've managed as as best we could to drag over from the West—and still we go on talking about independent Russian art! Some fine fellows have actually discovered original Russian science: with us, they say, twice two also makes four, but somehow it works out more briskly!'

'Come, come, Sozont Ivanitch!' Litvinov cried. 'Wait a minute! After all, we do send things to international exhibitions, and Europe does get certain supplies from us?'

'Yes, raw materials. And note: those raw materials are for the most part good just because of other things being bad. Thus, for instance, bristles are long and stiff because the pigs are poor; leather is thick and stout because the cows are thin; fat is rich because it's boiled down with half the flesh. . . . But I needn't go into details—you've studied technology, and must know all this better than I do. They keep talking of Russian inventiveness. Why, here are our landowners complaining bitterly and suffering loss because there doesn't exist a good machine for drying grain and they still have to put the sheaves into drying-sheds as in the times of Ryurik. Those drying-sheds are more trouble than they are worth, just like our bast shoes and mats, and they constantly catch fire. The land-owners complain, but the grain-drying machines are not forthcoming. And why aren't they? Because the Germans don't need them—they thresh the corn just as it's harvested and so they don't bother about inventing the machines—and we aren't equal to it! That's the long and short of it—we are incapable of it. I vow from to-day that as soon as I come across a born genius or a self-taught expert, I'll say to him: "Hey, where is the drying-machine? Produce it!" But that's beyond them! To pick up an old worn shoe, cast off ages ago by St. Simon or Fourier and, respectfully placing it on our heads, carry it about as a holy relic—that we can do right enough; or scribble an article about the historical and the present-day significance of the proletariat in the chief towns of France—that, too, comes easy to us. But when I asked one such scribbler and political economist—after the style of your Mr. Voroshilov—to name twenty towns in France, do you know what happened? The economist in despair ended by including Mont-Fermeuil among the French towns, recalling probably Paul de Kock's novel. That reminds me of something that once happened to me. I was making my way through a forest with a dog and a gun——'

'Are you a sportsman?' Litvinov asked.

'I go shooting now and again. I was looking for a marsh, in search of snipe; other sportsmen told me no end about that marsh. As I walked through a clearing I saw sitting in front of a hut a jolly-looking

young man, obviously a merchant's clerk; he sat
there grinning—for no reason that I could see. I
asked him where the marsh was, and whether there
were any snipe in it. "You're very welcome," he
spouted straight off, as pleased as though I'd pre-
sented him with a rouble, " delighted to be of service—
it's a first-rate marsh; and as to wildfowl of all kinds,
goodness me, the place is full of them." I went
on, but found no wildfowl of any description, and
indeed the marsh itself had dried up ages ago. Now
tell me, please, what does a Russian tell lies for?
Why does the political economist tell lies—also about
" wildfowl" ? '

Litvinov made no answer and only sighed in
sympathy.

' But if you talk to that same economist,' Potugin
went on, ' about the most difficult problems of social
science—in general, without asking for facts—fr-r-r-r!
he'll shoot up into the sky like a bird, a regular eagle.
I did manage once to catch such a bird: as you'll see,
I used a very good bait. I was talking to one of the
modern young men about various " questions " as
they call them. He was, of course, full of wrath and,
among other things, denounced marriage with truly
childish exasperation. I advanced all sorts of reasons
to him . . . no good! I saw there was no way of
getting at him. And suddenly a happy thought
struck me! " Allow me to observe, sir," I began—
one always has to speak respectfully to those young
men—" I am surprised at you: you study natural
science, but you've failed to notice that all predatory
and carnivorous animals, both beasts and birds, all

119

those who have to go in search of prey and to provide live food for themselves and their young—and you do include man among such animals, don't you?" "Of course I do," the young man said eagerly, "in fact, man is nothing but a carnivorous animal." "And a predatory one," I added. "Yes, and a predatory one," he confirmed. "Admirably put," I assented. "Well, so I am surprised at your failing to observe that all such animals are monogamous." The young man was startled. "How so?" "Well, they are. Think of the lion, the wolf, the fox, the hawk, the vulture. And indeed how could it be otherwise, if you'll kindly consider the matter: it's hard enough for the two parents to bring up their young." My young man pondered. "Well," he said, "in that case, a brute is no pattern for man." Thereupon I called him an idealist, and he was fearfully upset! He very nearly wept. I had to comfort him and tell him I wouldn't give him away to his comrades. To deserve the name of an idealist is no light matter! The point is, the young people of to-day are out of their reckoning. They imagine that the time for the old, obscure, underground work is over, that it was all very well for their elderly fathers to burrow like moles, but for them it would be humiliating to do so. "We'll work in the open, we'll take action!" they say. My dear young friends! not even your children will take action; and you'd better go down the mole-run again, in your fathers' footsteps!'

There was a pause.

'I do believe, my dear sir,' Potugin began again, 'that not only are we indebted to civilization for knowledge, art, law, but that the very feeling for beauty and poetry grows and develops under its influence; the so-called popular, naïve, unconscious art is sheer nonsense. In Homer one can already find traces of rich and refined culture; love itself is ennobled by it. The Slavophils would gladly hang me for such heresy if they weren't such kind-hearted creatures, but I insist on my point all the same. However much they may treat me to Madame Kohanovsky and *The Swarm at Rest*, I will not sniff this *triple extrait de moujik russe*, for I do not belong to the aristocracy which has from time to time to convince itself that it is not wholly frenchified. It is really for them that all that literature *en cuir de Russie* is composed. Try to read to a real peasant the most pithy, the most "popular" passages from *The Swarm*, and he will think that you are teaching him a new spell against fever or drunkenness. I repeat, without civilization there is no poetry. Do you want to know what is the poetic ideal of the uncivilized Russian? Read our legends, our *bylini*. I say nothing of the fact that love is always regarded in them as the result of magic, of spells and love-philtres, and is called witchery and enchantment; nor of the fact that our epic literature is the only one in the West and the East, mind you, the only one, not to have produced a typical pair of lovers—unless you count Vanka-Tanka.[1] The ancient Russian hero invariably begins his acquaintance with his bride-to-be by beating her on her white body with " his plaited whip "—" which keeps womankind soft and plump."

[1] The reference is to a popular song. (Translator's note.)

I will not speak of all that; but I should like to draw your attention to the elegant image of the young man, the *jeune-premier*, as it appeared to the primitive, uncivilized Slav. Look at him: the *jeune-premier* is walking along; "he has made for himself a marten fur coat, with fine close stitching down every seam, seven strands of silk make his woven belt, tied smooth and neat high above his waist; his fingers are hid by his smart long sleeves, the collar of his coat raised above his head, his ruddy face can't be seen for it, and his full white neck is hidden, too; his smart little cap he wears sideways, on his feet he has boots of leather fine, with points that curve and upstanding heels; round the pointed toes you can roll an egg, and a sparrow can fly between heel and sole." This fine young man walks with quick small steps like the Alcibiades of our legends, Tchurilo Plenkovitch, whose mincing gait had such an extraordinary, almost medicinal effect on old women and young girls. That is to the present day the gait of our waiters, who seem to be loose in every joint as they trot about with tiny steps—and they are the cream, the flower of purely Russian smartness, the *ne plus ultra* of Russian taste. I am not joking: clumsy jauntiness is our artistic ideal. A fine ideal, isn't it? It doesn't give much material for painting or sculpture, does it? And the beautiful maiden, who captivates the young man and is "as red in the face as the blood of a hare"! . . . But I believe you're not listening to me?'

Litvinov roused himself. He really had not heard what Potugin was saying: he was thinking, thinking all the time of Irina and their last meeting.

'Excuse me, Sozont Ivanitch,' he began, 'but I want to ask you the same old question ... about Madame Ratmirov.'

Potugin folded his newspaper and stuffed it into his pocket.

'You want again to know how I came to know her?'

'No, it isn't that; I should like to know what you think ... of the part she played in Petersburg. What was it exactly?'

'I hardly know what to say, Grigory Mihailitch. I came to know Madame Ratmirov rather intimately—but it was quite by chance and for a short time. I haven't tried to peep into her world, and what was happening there remained unknown to me. I heard rumours, but you know that with us gossip reigns not only in democratic circles. And, indeed, I didn't ask questions. But I see you're interested in her,' he added after a pause.

'Yes, we've had two rather candid talks. But I still keep asking myself, is she sincere?'

Potugin lowered his eyes. 'When she is carried away she is sincere, like all passionate women. Pride also sometimes prevents her from lying.'

'But is she proud? I should rather have thought, capricious.'

'Proud like the devil; but there's no harm in that.'

'It seems to me she sometimes exaggerates. . . .'

'There's no harm in that either; she is sincere all the same. But speaking generally, how can you expect truth? The best of those society women are spoiled to the marrow of their bones.'

'But, Sozont Ivanitch, you remember, you said

yourself you were a friend of hers. Why, you yourself brought me to her almost by force!'

'Well, what of it? She asked me to bring you, and
I thought, why not? And I really am her friend.
She has several good qualities: she is very kind, that
is, generous, that is, she gives to others what she
doesn't need entirely for herself. But no doubt you
know her quite as well as I do.'

'I knew Irina Pavlovna ten years ago, and since
then——'

'Eh, Grigory Mihailitch, what are you saying! As
though one's nature changed! What a man is in his
cradle, that he is on his deathbed. Or maybe—'
Potugin bent his head still lower—'maybe you're
afraid of falling into her hands? There is that danger
of course. . . . But there is no escaping some woman's
hands, you know.'

Litvinov gave a forced laugh. 'You think so?'

'There's no escaping. Human nature is weak,
woman is strong, chance is all-powerful; it's hard to
resign oneself to a colourless existence, it's impossible
to renounce oneself altogether . . . and here is beauty
and kindness and warmth and light—so how can one
resist? Why, one runs like a child to its nurse. And
afterwards, of course, comes cold and darkness and
emptiness . . . all in its proper order. And in the end
one gets out of touch with everything, ceases to
understand anything. At first it will seem incomprehensible how one can love; afterwards, how one
can live at all.'

Litvinov looked at Potugin and it seemed to him
that he had never yet met a man more lonely, more

forsaken . . . more unhappy. This time he was not being shy or constrained: pale and downcast, hanging his head and resting his hands on his knees, he sat quite still and only smiled a mournful smile. Litvinov felt sorry for the strange, embittered man.

'Irina Pavlovna mentioned to me in conversation,' he began in an undertone, 'a close friend of hers whose name was Belsky or Dolsky if I remember rightly. . . .'

Potugin raised his sad little eyes.

'Oh!' he said in a toneless voice. 'She mentioned . . . well, and what of it? But it's time I was going home,' he added with a forced yawn, 'to dinner. Good-bye.'

He suddenly got up from the seat and walked away before Litvinov had time to utter a word. Litvinov's feeling of pity gave way to vexation—vexation with himself, of course. Indiscretion was not at all in his character; he had meant to express his sympathy for Potugin, but instead had made something like an awkward hint. He returned to his hotel with an uneasy heart.

'Spoiled to the marrow of her bones,' he thought a little later, 'proud as the devil! She, that woman, who was almost on her knees before me? Proud, and not capricious?'

Litvinov tried to banish Irina from his mind but did not succeed. He deliberately avoided thinking of his betrothed: he felt that Irina's image would not give way to any other that day. He decided not to worry but to wait for the solution of all this 'strange business'; the solution was bound to come soon, and Litvinov had not the least doubt that it would be quite harmless and natural. That was what he thought, and meanwhile not only was Irina's image always before him, but every word she had uttered kept in turn recurring in his memory.

The waiter brought him a note: it too was from Irina.

'If you have nothing to do this evening, will you come: I shall not be alone, I have visitors—and you will see our set, our society, at still closer range. I very much want you to see them; I fancy they will show themselves in all their brilliance. After all, you ought to know what air I breathe. Do come; I shall be glad to see you, and I think you won't be bored. Prove to me that our explanation to-day has once for all made any misunderstanding between us impossible. Yours ever, Irina.'

Litvinov put on a tail-coat and white tie and went to Irina's. 'There's nothing in it,' he said to himself on the way, 'and as to having a look at *them*—why not? It's interesting.' A few days ago he had felt differently about those people: they had roused his indignation.

He walked fast, his hat over his eyes, and a constrained smile on his lips, while Bambaev, sitting in front of Weber's Café and pointing him out from a distance to Pishchalkin and Voroshilov, exclaimed enthusiastically: 'Do you see that man? He's a stone! He's a rock! He's granite!'

XV

LITVINOV found a good many visitors at Irina's. Three of the generals whom he had met at the picnic— the stout, the irritable, and the indulgent one—were sitting at a card-table in a corner playing dummy whist. Human language has no words to express the dignity with which they dealt, won tricks, led clubs, led diamonds . . . they were statesmen indeed! Leaving to the small fry, *aux bourgeois*, the jokes and proverbial sayings usual at cards, the generals uttered only the strictly necessary words; the stout general, however, allowed himself between two deals to utter with much vigour: ' *Ce satané as de pique!* ' Litvinov recognized some of the ladies he had seen at the picnic, but there were others who were new to him. There was one lady so old that it seemed she would fall to pieces any moment; she moved her bare, horrible, dark-grey shoulders and, covering her mouth with her fan, languidly squinted at Ratmirov with utterly lifeless eyes. He was very attentive to her: she was much respected in high circles as the last lady-in-waiting of the Empress Catherine. Countess S., ' the Queen of the Wasps,' dressed like a shepherdess, sat by the window surrounded by a crowd of young men; among them Finikov, famous for his wealth and good looks, attracted attention by his arrogant bearing, flat skull, and soullessly brutal expression, worthy of a Khan of Bokhara or a Roman Heliogabalus. Another lady, also a countess, known shortly as Lise, was talking to a pale 'spiritualist' with long fair hair; a gentleman, also pale and long-haired, stood beside them, laughing significantly now and again: this gentleman also believed in spiritualism, but he went in for prophecy as well and, on the basis of the Revelation and the Talmud, predicted all sorts of wonderful events; not one of those events ever happened, but he was not abashed and went on prophesying. The 'born genius' who aroused such indignation in Potugin sat at the piano striking an occasional chord *d'une main distraite* and negligently looking about him.

Irina was sitting on the sofa between Prince Kokó and Mme X, once a famous beauty and a national fountain of wisdom, who had long since turned into a shrivelled-up toadstool smelling of Lenten oil and evaporated poison. Irina blushed when she saw Litvinov, got up from her seat, and when he came up to her, warmly shook hands with him. She was wearing a dress of black crêpe with scarcely perceptible gold trimmings; her shoulders were of a pearly whiteness, and her face, pale under the sudden flush that overspread it, breathed of triumphant beauty—and not of beauty only: a secret, almost derisive joy shone in her half-closed eyes, fluttered round her lips and nostrils . . .

Ratmirov came up to Litvinov and, exchanging with him the usual greetings—without his usual playfulness, however—introduced him to two or three ladies: to the old ruin, the Queen of the Wasps,

Countess Lise. . . . They received him quite favourably.
Litvinov did not belong to their set . . . but he was
distinctly good-looking, and his young, expressive
face attracted their attention.   He did not, however,
succeed in retaining it: he was not used to society and
felt rather shy, and to make matters worse the stout
general stared at him persistently.   'Aha, the rebel,
the freethinker!' his fixed, heavy gaze seemed to say,
'so you've come cap in hand, have you, dancing
attendance on us?'

Irina came to his rescue.   She managed so cleverly
that he found himself in the corner close by the door,
a little behind her.   Every time she spoke to him she
had to turn round, and every time he admired the
beautiful curve of her glossy neck and breathed in the
delicate fragrance of her hair.   An expression of
gratitude, gentle and profound, did not leave her
face: he could not help recognizing that it really was
gratitude her glances and smiles expressed—and he
too overflowed with the same feeling, and his heart
was filled with contrition and sweetness and dread. . . .
And at the same time, it was as though she wanted
to say 'Well, what do you think of them?'   That
unspoken question was particularly clear to Litvinov
whenever one of the guests said or did something
vulgar, which happened more than once during the
evening.   On one occasion she could not restrain
herself and laughed aloud.

Countess Lise, a highly superstitious lady with a
bent for the extraordinary, having talked to her heart's
content with the fair-headed spiritualist about Home,
turning tables, accordions that played of themselves,

and so on, ended by asking him if there were any animals that could be affected by magnetism.

'One such animal certainly exists,' Prince Kokó responded from the other end of the room. 'You know Milvanovsky, don't you? He was sent into hypnotic sleep in my presence and he actually snored!'

'You are very malicious, *mon prince*, I am speaking of real animals, *je parle des bêtes.*'

'*Mais moi aussi, madame, je parle d'une bête.*'

'There are real animals too,' the spiritualist intervened, 'for instance, crabs; they are very sensitive and easily fall into the cataleptic state.'

The countess was very much surprised. 'What! Crabs! Indeed? Oh, that's awfully interesting! I should like to see that. M'sieur Luzhin . . .' she said addressing a young man with a face as stony as a new doll's and an equally stony collar. (He was renowned for having exposed his face and his collar to the spray of Niagara and the Nubian Nile, but he remembered nothing of his travels and only cared for Russian puns.) 'M'sieur Luzhin, would you be so kind as to get a crab for us?'

Monsieur Luzhin grinned.

'Do you mean "look lively!" or a live one?' he asked.

The countess failed to understand him. '*Mais oui*, a crab,' she repeated, '*une écrevisse.*'

'What, what's that? A crab? A crab?' Countess S. sternly intervened. She was annoyed at the absence of Monsieur Verdier: she could not understand why Irina had not invited that most charming of Frenchmen.

The ruin was past understanding anything, and,

besides, her deafness was getting too much for her, so
she merely shook her head.

'*Oui, oui, vous allez voir*. M'sieur Luzhin, please. . . .'

The young traveller bowed, went out of the room,
and soon came back followed by a waiter who,
smiling broadly, carried a dish with a big black crab
on it.

'*Voici, madame!*' Luzhin exclaimed. 'Now we
can begin crabbing the crab. Ha-ha-ha!' (Russians
are always the first to laugh at their own witticisms.)

'He-he-he!' responded Prince Kokó as a patriot
and champion of all home produce.

(We beg the readers not to be surprised or indignant: who can vouch that he has not applauded even
worse puns as he sat in the stalls of the Alexandrinsky
Theatre, infected by its atmosphere?)

'*Merci, merci*,' said the countess. '*Allons, allons,
monsieur Fox, montrez-nous ça.*'

The waiter put the dish on a round table. There
was a slight movement among the guests; several
heads turned round; only the generals at the card-table
preserved the sedate dignity of their pose. The
spiritualist ruffled his hair, frowned, and approaching
the table began making passes in the air. The crab
stirred, backed, and raised its claws. The spiritualist
made the passes quicker and more frequently: the
crab behaved as before.

'*Mais que doit-elle donc faire?*' the countess asked.

'*Elle doâ rester immobile et se dresser sur sa quiou,*'
Mr. Fox answered with a strong American accent,
waving his hands convulsively over the dish;
but magnetism had no effect, the crab went on

moving. The spiritualist declared that it was one of his bad days, and turned away from the table, looking annoyed. The countess tried to console him, saying that Home himself had similar failures. . . . Prince Kokó confirmed her words. The authority on the Talmud and the Revelation went up to the table on the quiet and making quick and vigorous thrusts with his fingers also tried his luck, but it was no good: the crab showed no signs of catalepsy. Then the waiter was called in and asked to carry the crab away. He did so with the same broad grin and was heard to guffaw behind the door. Afterwards they laughed a great deal in the kitchen *über diese Russen*.

During the experiment with the crab the 'born genius' went on striking chords at the piano, chiefly in a minor key, for one can never tell what effect a thing may have; now he played his invariable waltz, received, of course, with most flattering approval. Moved by rivalry, Count X, our incomparable dilettante (see Chapter I), 'recited' a *chansonnette* of his own invention, filched entirely from Offenbach. Its playful refrain to the words '*Quel œuf? quel bœuf?*' made almost all the ladies move their heads right and left to measure; one actually gave a slight moan of delight and the irrefutable, inevitable word '*Charmant! Charmant!*' was on the lips of all. Irina exchanged looks with Litvinov and again that secret, mocking expression played round her mouth. It was still more pronounced and indeed grew almost malicious when a little later Prince Kokó, the champion and representative of the rights of nobility, took it into his head to expound his ideas to the spiritualist. Of course, he immediately made use of his famous phrase about the foundations of private property being shaken in Russia and said a few unpleasant things about democracy. The spiritualist's American blood was roused: he began to argue. The prince, as usual, at once started shouting for all he was worth, continually repeating, instead of any arguments, '*C'est absurde! cela n'a pas le sens commun!*' The millionaire Finikov began making insulting remarks all round; the Talmudist's voice became a squeak, the Countess S. almost screeched. . . . In short there was the same kind of absurd uproar as at Gubaryov's, except that there was no beer and no tobacco smoke, and the people were better dressed. Ratmirov tried to restore peace (the generals expressed displeasure, Boris was heard to exclaim: '*Encore cette satanée politique!* ') but met with no success. One of the guests, a high official of the mildly insidious variety, undertook to make '*le résumé de la question en peu de mots,*' and he failed also; indeed it could not have been otherwise, for he obviously did not himself grasp what *la question* was, hesitated, repeated himself, and was utterly incapable of either listening to objections or understanding them. To make matters worse Irina slyly goaded on the disputants and set them against one another, continually turning round to Litvinov and slightly nodding to him. . . . And he sat there like one bewitched, hearing nothing, and only waiting for another flash from those magnificent eyes, for another glimpse of that pale, tender, malicious, charming face. . . .

Finally, the ladies rebelled and demanded that the

discussion should stop. Ratmirov persuaded the dilettante to repeat his *chansonnette*, and the 'born genius' played his waltz once more.

Litvinov stayed till past midnight and was the last to leave. In the course of the evening the conversation touched upon a number of topics, carefully avoiding anything in the least interesting. The generals joined in it majestically when they had finished their majestic game; the influence of those statesmen made itself felt at once. The conversation turned to the stars of the Parisian *demi-monde* whose names and talents proved to be well known to every one; they talked of the last play by Sardou, a novel by About, of Patti in *La Traviata*. Someone offered to play 'post,' *au secrétaire*, but that was not a success. Many of the answers were flat and not without grammatical mistakes. The stout general told of how he once had answered the question '*Qu'est ce que l'amour?*' by saying '*Une colique remontée au cœur,*' and immediately laughed his wooden laugh; the ruin struck him sharply on the hand with her fan; a piece of make-up was shaken off her forehead by this sudden movement. The withered toadstool said something about the Slav principalities and the need for Orthodox propaganda beyond the Danube, but evoking no response hissed and subsided. On the whole they talked most about Home; the 'Queen of the Wasps' herself described how she saw hands creeping over her and how she put her own ring on the finger of one of them.

It was indeed a triumph for Irina: even if Litvinov had paid more attention to what was being said, he could not have picked out a single sincere word, a single sensible idea or new fact from all that dull and incoherent babble. There was no real excitement in their shouts and exclamations, no passion in their censure: only sometimes the fear of financial loss found vent in a querulous squeak escaping from under the mask of public-spirited indignation or contemptuous indifference; and a few names that will be gratefully remembered by posterity were uttered with gnashing of teeth. . . . And not a drop of living water under all this litter and rubbish! What stale trash, what worthless trifles, what barren futilities occupied all those hearts and minds—and not only on that particular evening, not only in society, but in their homes, at all days and hours, throughout the breadth and depth of their existence! And, at bottom, what ignorance! What lack of understanding of all that human life is built upon and of all that adorns it!

Taking leave of Litvinov Irina again pressed his hand and whispered significantly: 'Well? Are you satisfied? Have you seen enough? Fine, isn't it?' He did not answer but only made a low and silent bow.

Left alone with her husband Irina was about to go into her bedroom. . . . He stopped her.

'*Je vous ai beaucoup admiré ce soir, madame,*' he said, leaning against the mantlepiece and lighting a cigarette. '*Vous vous êtes parfaitement moquée de nous tous.*'

'*Pas plus cette fois-ci que les autres,*' she answered indifferently.

' How am I to understand that? ' Ratmirov asked.

' As you like.'

' Hm. *C'est clair.*' With a careful cat-like movement Ratmirov shook off his cigarette ash with the
long nail of his little finger. ' By the way, that new
friend of yours—what's his name? . . . Mr. Litvinov
—has probably the reputation of being highly intelligent.'

At Litvinov's name Irina quickly turned round.

' What do you mean? '

The general smiled ironically.

' He is very silent—evidently afraid to compromise
himself.'

Irina smiled too, but in a different way.

' Better be silent than talk . . . like some people.'

Attrapé! ' Ratmirov said with assumed humility.
' But joking apart, he has a very interesting face.
Such a . . . such an intent expression . . . and, indeed,
his whole bearing. . . . Yes.' The general straightened
his cravat, and throwing back his head looked at his
own moustache. ' I expect he is a republican, like
that other friend of yours, Mr. Potugin; he's one of
those tongue-tied intelligent people too.'

Irina slowly raised her eyebrows over her light,
wide open eyes and slightly pursed up her lips.

' What's the point of your saying this, Valerian
Vladimirovitch?' she said with apparent sympathy.
' It's simply wasting your shot in the air. . . . We
are not in Russia and no one hears you.'

Ratmirov winced.

' It's not only my opinion, Irina Pavlovna,' he
said in an unexpectedly high-pitched guttural voice;

136

'other people too think that that gentleman looks like a revolutionary.'

'Indeed? And who are those others?'

'Why, Boris, for instance——'

'What? Did that man too think fit to express an opinion?' Irina moved her shoulders as though shrinking from the cold and softly passed the tips of her fingers over them.

'That man . . . yes, that man. . . . Allow me to observe that you seem to be angry, Irina Pavlovna, and you know yourself, if one is angry——'

'Angry? Why should I be?'

'I don't know; perhaps you've been upset by the remark I've ventured to make, about——'

Ratmirov hesitated.

'About what?' Irina asked. 'Please, no irony and be quick, I am tired and sleepy.' She took up the candle from the table. 'What is it?'

'Why, about that Mr. Litvinov. Since there isn't the slightest doubt now that you're greatly interested in him——'

Irina raised the hand in which she held the candlestick, so that the flame of the candle was on the level with her husband's face, and, looking into his eyes attentively and almost with curiosity, suddenly burst out laughing.

'What's the matter?' Ratmirov asked with a frown. Irina went on laughing.

'But what is it?' he asked, stamping his foot. He felt stung, insulted, and at the same time the beauty of this woman who stood before him so lightly and confidently struck him against his will—it tortured

137

him. He saw the whole of her, all her charms, down to the rosy gloss of the elegant nails on the slender fingers that firmly clasped the dark bronze of the heavy candlestick—even that gloss did not escape his eye ... and the injury sank deeper and deeper into his heart. Irina was still laughing.

'What? You? You are jealous?' she uttered at last, and turning her back on her husband went out of the room. 'He is jealous!' he heard her say behind the doors, and her laugh rang out again.

Ratmirov followed her gloomily with his eyes— and once more he could not help noticing the bewitching grace of her figure, of all her movements. Crushing his cigarette against the marble mantelpiece he flung it far away from him. His cheeks suddenly turned pale, a spasm passed over his chin, and his eyes, dull and savage, scanned the floor as though looking for something. His face lost all semblance of refinement. It must have worn a similar expression when he was flogging the peasants in White Russia.

Litvinov meanwhile returned to his room and sitting down in front of the table and resting his head on his hands remained motionless. At last he stood up, opened a drawer, and taking out his pocket-book drew out of an inner pocket Tatyana's photograph. Altered and, as usual, aged by the photograph, her face looked at him mournfully. Litvinov's betrothed was a girl of Great-Russian stock, fair-haired, rather plump, and with somewhat heavy features but with a wonderful expression of goodness and gentleness in the intelligent hazel eyes, and a white, tender brow on which a ray of sunshine seemed to rest. Litvinov gazed at the photograph long and intently; then he slowly moved it to one side and clutched his head again with both hands. 'It's all over,' he murmured at last. 'Irina! Irina!'

It was only then, only at that moment, he understood that he had fallen in love with her madly and irreme-diably, had fallen in love on the very first day he met her at the Old Castle, that he had never ceased to love her. And yet how surprised, how incredulous, and perhaps amused he would have been had someone told him so a few hours before.

'But Tanya, Tanya, good God! Tanya!' he repeated in contrition; and meanwhile the image of Irina rose before him in her black, as it were mourning, raiment, with the radiant calm of victory on her marble-white face.

XVI

LITVINOV did not sleep all night and did not undress.
He felt very unhappy. As an honest and conscientious
man he understood the importance of obligations and
the sacredness of duty; he would have been ashamed
to prevaricate with himself about his weakness, his
failure. At first a kind of stupor came upon him;
he could not free himself from the oppressive weight
of one vague, half-conscious feeling. Then he was
possessed by horror at the thought that the future,
the future he had almost won for himself, was again
lost in darkness, that his house, his secure, freshly
built house, suddenly tottered. . . . He began reproach-
ing himself pitilessly, but pulled himself up at once.
'That's weak of me,' he thought. 'It's not a time
for reproaches, I must act. Tanya is my betrothed,
she has trusted my love, my honour, we are bound
together for life and cannot, must not, part.'

He vividly pictured to himself all Tatyana's qualities,
he dwelt upon them and counted them over; he tried
to rouse love and tenderness in himself. 'The only
thing that remains,' he thought again, 'is to run
away, at once, without waiting for her arrival, to
hasten to meet her. I may suffer, I may be wretched
with Tanya—though that's unlikely—but anyway I
mustn't think of that; I must do my duty, even if I die

after it!' 'But you have no right to deceive her,' another voice whispered to him. 'You have no right to conceal from her the change in your feelings; maybe she will not want to be your wife when she knows that you have fallen in love with another woman.' 'Nonsense, nonsense!' he retorted, 'that's mere sophistry, shameful prevarication, false conscientiousness; I have no right not to keep my word, that's certain. Very well—then I must leave here without seeing the other. . . .'

But when he said that his heart ached with anguish and he felt cold, physically cold; a momentary shiver ran down his body and his teeth chattered. He stretched himself and yawned as though in a fever. Without dwelling on his last idea, stifling it and turning away from it, he began wondering how he could again . . . again fall in love with that spoiled society woman in her hateful, hostile surroundings. He tried to ask himself: 'But come, are you really in love?' and at once dismissed the question with a wave of his hand. He was still wondering and marvelling, and meanwhile, as though from soft and fragrant mists, the enchanting image rose before him, the long silky lashes were lifted—and the magical eyes gently and irresistibly pierced his heart, the voice rang out sweetly, and the resplendent shoulders, the shoulders of a young queen, breathed of freshness and languorous ardour.

Towards morning a decision had ripened in Litvinov's mind. He resolved to leave that very day and go to meet Tatyana, to see Irina for the last time, tell

141

her, if necessary, the whole truth—and part from her for ever.

He put his things in order and packed them, waited till twelve o'clock, and went to Irina's. But at the sight of her half-curtained windows his heart failed him . . . he had not the spirit to go into the hotel. He took several turns up and down the Lichtenthal Avenue. 'My respects to Mr. Litvinov!' an ironical voice called from the top of a rapidly moving dogcart. Litvinov raised his eyes and saw General Ratmirov sitting next to Prince M., the well-known sportsman, keen on English horses and carriages. The prince was driving, and the general, bending over to one side, was holding his hat high above his head and grinning. Litvinov bowed to him and immediately, as though obeying a secret command, ran to Irina's.

She was at home. He sent in his name and was received at once. When he came in she was standing in the middle of the room. She was wearing a morning dress with wide open sleeves; her face, pale as yesterday, but not as fresh, looked tired; the languid smile with which she welcomed her guest made this more apparent. She held out her hand to him and looked at him kindly, but absent-mindedly.

'Thank you for coming,' she said in a plaintive voice, sinking into an arm-chair. 'I am not quite well to-day; I had a bad night. Well, what do you say about last night? Wasn't I right?'

Litvinov sat down.

'I've come to you, Irina Pavlovna——' he began.

She instantly drew herself up and turned to him:
her eyes fixed him intently.

'What's the matter with you?' she exclaimed.
'You are pale as death—you are ill.   What is it?'

Litvinov was confused.

'What's the matter with me, Irina Pavlovna?'

'Have you had bad news?   Has something dreadful
happened?   Tell me, tell me. . . .'

Litvinov in his turn looked at Irina.

'I've had no bad news,' he brought out with some
effort, 'but something dreadful really has happened,
a great misfortune—and that's what's brought me
here.'

'A misfortune?   What misfortune?'

'Why, this——'

Litvinov wanted to go on, but he could not.   He
only clenched his hands so that his fingers cracked.
Irina bent forward and seemed turned to stone.

'Oh, I love you!' broke out at last in a stifled
moan from Litvinov's breast, and he turned away as
though wishing to hide his face.

'What, Grigory Mihailitch, you——' Irina could
not finish the sentence either, and leaning back in the
chair raised both her hands to her eyes.   'You—
love me?'

'Yes . . . yes . . . yes . . .' he repeated with exasperation, turning his face away more and more.

All was still in the room: a stray butterfly was
fluttering its wings as it struggled between the curtain
and the window-pane.

Litvinov was the first to speak.

'That, Irina Pavlovna,' he began, 'that is the

misfortune which . . . has befallen me. I ought to have foreseen and avoided it, had I not been caught in the whirlpool all of a sudden, as in those Moscow days. Evidently the fates willed that I should suffer once more, and again through you, the torments which, one would have thought, had been done with for ever. It was with good reason that I resisted . . . tried to resist; but, apparently, there's no escaping one's fate. I am telling you all this so as to make haste and end this . . . tragic comedy,' he added with a new access of exasperation and shame.

Litvinov was silent again; the butterfly was struggling and fluttering as before. Irina did not take her hands away from her face.

'And you are sure you're not mistaken?' her whisper came from under those white, almost bloodless hands.

'I am not mistaken,' Litvinov answered in a toneless voice. 'I love you as I've never loved any one but you. I won't reproach you, that would be too absurd; I won't repeat to you that perhaps nothing of this would have happened had you treated me differently. . . . Of course, I alone am to blame, my self-confidence ruined me; it serves me right, and you could not possibly have expected it. Of course it hasn't occurred to you that it would have been far safer for me had you been less conscious of having wronged me—as you fancy you did—and less anxious to make up for it . . . but what's done can't be undone. I merely wanted to explain my position to you—it's hard enough as it is . . . at any rate there will be no more misunderstandings, as you put it, and

I hope the frankness of my confession will make you feel less offended with me than you are bound to feel.'

Litvinov spoke without raising his eyes; and even if he had looked at Irina he could not have seen her expression, for she was still covering her face with her hands. But the changes that passed over it would probably have surprised him: there was fear in her face, and joy, and anxiety, and a kind of blissful exhaustion; her eyes shone faintly from under drooping eyelids, and her uneven, drawn-out breath was chill upon her parched, half-open lips.

Litvinov paused, waiting for a response, for a sound. . . . There was nothing.

' The only thing left me,' he began again, ' is to go away. I've come to say good-bye.'

Irina slowly dropped her hands on her knees. ' But if I remember rightly, Grigory Mihailitch,' she began, ' the—the person you mentioned was to have come here. Aren't you expecting her? '

' Yes; but I'll write to her . . . she will stop somewhere on the way . . . say, at Heidelberg.'

'Ah, at Heidelberg. . . . Yes—it's a nice place. . . . But all this must be upsetting your plans. Are you sure, Grigory Mihailitch, that you don't exaggerate, *et que ce n'est pas une fausse alarme*? '

Irina spoke quietly and almost coldly, pausing occasionally and looking away, at the window. Litvinov did not answer her last question.

' Only why did you speak of my being offended? ' she went on. ' I am not . . . oh, no ! And if either of us is to blame, it's certainly not you; not you

alone. . . . Recall our last conversations and you will
see it wasn't your fault.'

'I've never doubted your magnanimity,' Litvinov
said through his teeth, 'but I'd like to know if you
approve of my intention.'

'To go away?'

'Yes.'

Irina was still looking away from him.

'At first your decision seemed to me premature . . .
but now I've thought over what you said . . . and if
you really are not mistaken, I think you ought to go.
It will be better so . . . better for both of us.'

Irina's voice grew lower and lower and she spoke
more and more slowly.

'General Ratmirov might certainly notice——'
Litvinov began. Irina looked down again, and a
strange flicker passed over her lips for an instant.

'No you didn't understand me,' she interrupted
him. 'I wasn't thinking of my husband. Why
should I? There wouldn't have been anything for
him to notice. But I repeat; parting is essential for
us both.'

Litvinov picked up his hat that had fallen on the
floor. 'All is over,' he thought, 'I must go. So
it remains to me to bid you good-bye, Irina Pavlovna,'
he said aloud, and a dread came upon him, as though
he was going to pass sentence on himself. 'All I
may hope for is that you will not remember evil
against me . . . and that if we ever——'

Irina interrupted him again.

'Wait, Grigory Mihailitch, don't say good-bye to
me yet. It would be too sudden.'

Something seemed to give way in Litvinov but burning bitterness flooded his heart again with redoubled force.

'But I can't stay !' he cried out. 'What's the good? Why prolong this misery?'

'Don't say good-bye to me yet,' Irina repeated. 'I must see you once more. . . . Another such dumb parting as in Moscow . . . no, I don't want that. You can go now, but you must promise me, promise on your honour, that you won't go without seeing me again.'

'You wish it?'

'I insist on it. If you go away without saying good-bye to me, I shall never, never forgive it to you, do you hear: never! It's strange,' she added as though to herself, 'I can't believe that I am in Baden . . . I keep fancying I am in Moscow. . . . Go.'

Litvinov got up.

'Irina Pavlovna, give me your hand,' he said.

Irina shook her head.

'I told you I don't want to say good-bye.'

'It isn't to say good-bye that I ask for it. . . .'

Irina stretched out her hand, but after looking at Litvinov—for the first time after his avowal—she drew it back.

'No, no,' she whispered, 'I won't give you my hand. No . . . no. You must go.'

Litvinov bowed and went out. He could not know why Irina refused him the last friendly hand-shake. . . . He could not know what it was she feared.

He went out, and Irina sank into the arm-chair once more and again covered her face with her hands.

XVII

LITVINOV did not go home: he went to the hills and getting into a thicket of trees threw himself on the ground, face downwards, and lay there for about an hour. He did not fret or weep; he seemed to swoon slowly and painfully. He had never experienced anything like it: it was an unendurable gnawing sensation of emptiness, emptiness within and without, all around him. . . . He thought neither of Irina nor of Tatyana. All he felt was that the blow had fallen and life was snapped in two like a cord, and he was caught and carried away by something cold and unknown. Sometimes he fancied that a whirlwind had swooped down upon him and he was conscious of the rapid beating and the tempestuous impact of its dark wings. . . . But his decision was unshaken. To remain in Baden . . . that was out of the question. In his mind he had left it already: he was already sitting in a noisy and smoky railway carriage, running away, away, into the dumb and desolate distance. He sat up at last and leaning his head against a tree remained motionless, except that he unconsciously took hold with one hand of a topmost frond of bracken and moved it rhythmically to and fro.

The sound of approaching footsteps roused him from his stupor: two charcoal-burners with big sacks on their shoulders were making their way down the steep footpath. 'It's time,' Litvinov whispered, and, following them, walked into the town. He turned in the direction of the railway station and sent off a telegram to Tatyana's aunt, Kapitolina Markovna, saying that he was leaving at once and asking them to meet him at Schrader's Hotel at Heidelberg. 'I may as well end it at once,' he thought, 'it's no use putting it off till to-morrow.' Then he went into the gambling-hall, looked with dull curiosity into two or three gamblers' faces, noticed in the distance Bindasov's detestable head, Pishchalkin's irreproachable countenance, and after standing for a little while in the colonnade, walked leisurely to Irina's. It was not under the influence of a sudden involuntary impulse that he went to her; having decided to go away, he also decided to keep his promise to her and see her once more. He entered the hotel unnoticed by the hall-porter, walked up the stairs not meeting any one, and without knocking at the door mechanically pushed it open and walked in. Irina was in the room, in the same dress, in the same arm-chair, in the same position as he had left her three hours before. One could see she had not got up or moved all this time. She slowly raised her head and, seeing Litvinov, shuddered all over and clutched at the arm of the chair. 'You frightened me,' she whispered.

Litvinov gazed at her in silent amazement. The expression of her face, of her lustreless eyes, gave him a shock.

Irina smiled with an effort and tidied her loosened hair. 'It's nothing. . . . I really don't know . . . I think I must have fallen asleep.'

'Excuse my coming unannounced,' Litvinov began. 'I wanted to fulfil the request you chose to make. As I am going away to-day——'

'To-day? But I believe you said you were going to write a letter first——'

'I sent a telegram.'

'Ah! You thought fit to hurry. And when are you going? At what time, I mean?'

'At seven in the evening.'

'Ah, at seven! And you've come to say good-bye?'

'Yes, to say good-bye.'

Irina paused.

'I must thank you, Grigory Mihailitch; you probably didn't find it easy to come here.'

'No, not easy at all, Irina Pavlovna.'

'Life isn't easy altogether, is it? What do you think?'

'That depends.'

Irina paused again; she seemed lost in thought.

'You have proved your friendship for me by coming,' she brought out at last. 'Thank you. And altogether I approve of your decision to end everything as soon as possible . . . because every delay . . . because . . . because I—I whom you've accused of coquetry and called a comedian—that, I believe, was the word you used?'

Irina got up quickly and moving to another chair, bent down, and pressed her hands and face to the edge of the table.

'Because I love you . . .' she whispered through her clenched fingers. Litvinov staggered as though someone had struck him in the chest. Irina dejectedly turned her head away from him as though now she, too, wanted to hide her face from him, and rested it against the table.

'Yes, I love you . . . I love you . . . and you know it.'

'I? I know it?' Litvinov brought out at last.

'Well, and now you see,' Irina went on, 'that you really must go away, that you mustn't delay . . . neither you nor I can afford to delay. It's dangerous, it's frightening. . . . Good-bye!' she added impulsively, getting up from her chair. 'Good-bye!'

She took a few steps towards her boudoir door and stretching out her hand behind her, rapidly moved it in the air as though wishing to meet and press Litvinov's hand; but he stood at a distance, rooted to the spot. She said once more: 'Good-bye, forget me,' and without looking back rushed out of the room.

Litvinov was left alone, but could not recover his senses. He came to himself at last, and walking with quick steps to the boudoir door called Irina's name once, twice, three times. . . . He had his hand on the door handle when he heard General Ratmirov's sonorous voice at the front door of the hotel.

Litvinov pulled down his hat over his eyes and went out. The elegant general was standing in front of the hall-porter's lobby, explaining to the man in bad German that he wanted to hire a carriage for the whole of the day. Seeing Litvinov he again expressed his 'respects' and raised his hat unnaturally high over his head; he was obviously making fun of him, but Litvinov had no thoughts to spare for that. He scarcely returned Ratmirov's greeting, and, on reaching his lodging, stopped in front of his portmanteau, which was already packed and fastened. His head was reeling and his heart vibrated like a string. What was he to do? And could he have foreseen it?

Yes, he had foreseen it, incredible as it seemed. It came like a thunderbolt, but he had foreseen it though he did not dare to confess it to himself. Though indeed he knew nothing for certain. Everything in him was entangled and confused; he lost the thread of his own thoughts. He recalled Moscow, he recalled how then, too, 'it' came upon him like a sudden storm. He was breathless: ecstasy, but hopeless and comfortless, was raging in his heart and almost choking him. He would not for anything in the world have agreed that Irina's words had remained unsaid . . . and yet those words could not alter his decision. It was unshakable as before and stood firm like an anchor. Litvinov lost the thread of his thoughts . . . yes; but his will was still his own and he disposed of himself as of another man, his subordinate. He rang for the waiter, asked for his bill, reserved a seat in the evening omnibus; he deliberately cut off every avenue of escape. 'Even if I die afterwards,' he said to himself over and over again as he had done during his sleepless night; that phrase particularly pleased him. 'Even if I die afterwards,' he repeated walking slowly up and down the room. But now and again Irina's words invaded his heart and burned it as with fire, and then he involuntarily closed his eyes and held his breath. 'Evidently one cannot love twice,' he thought, 'another life has entered into you, you've let it in—and you can't get

rid of the poison to the end of your life, you cannot break those bonds! That's so, but what of it? Happiness . . . but is it possible? You love her, that's true . . . and she . . . she loves you. . . .'

But at this point he had to take himself in hand again. Just as a traveller on a dark night, afraid of losing his way, does not lose sight for a moment of a light he sees in the distance, so Litvinov constantly fixed his attention on one point, on one aim. To appear before his betrothed, or rather (he tried not to think of his betrothed) to appear in the room of the Heidelberg hotel—that was his lodestar, his guiding light. What would happen afterwards he did not know and did not want to know. . . . One thing was certain: he was not coming back. 'Even if I die afterwards,' he repeated for the tenth time and glanced at the clock.

A quarter past six! How long he still had to wait! He began pacing up and down the room again. The sun was about to set, the sky above the trees glowed red, and crimson twilight streamed through the narrow windows into his darkened room. Suddenly Litvinov fancied that the door behind him opened quickly and noiselessly, and closed as quickly . . . he turned round: a woman wrapped in a black cloak was standing by the door. . . .

'Irina!' he cried clasping his hands.

She raised her head and fell upon his breast.

Two hours later he was sitting on the sofa in his room. His portmanteau, unpacked and empty, stood in the corner, and on the table, among his things scattered in disorder, lay a letter from Tatyana which had only just come. She wrote to say that as her aunt had completely recovered, they had decided to leave Dresden sooner than they had thought, and, all being well, would arrive at Baden at twelve o'clock the following day; they hoped that he would meet them at the station. Litvinov had already engaged rooms for them in his hotel.

That same evening he sent a note to Irina, and the following morning received an answer from her. ' A day sooner or a day later,' she wrote, 'it was inevitable. And I repeat to you what I said yesterday: my life is in your hands, do with me what you will. I don't want to hamper your freedom, but I want to tell you that if need be I will throw up everything and follow you to the ends of the earth. We shall see each other to-morrow, shan't we? Your Irina.'

The last two words were written in a large, sweeping, resolute hand.

XVIII

By twelve o'clock on 18th August Litvinov was among the people gathered at the railway station. Shortly before he arrived there he met Irina: she was sitting in an open carriage with her husband and another gentleman. She saw Litvinov and he noticed it; her eyes grew dark for an instant, but she immediately screened herself from him with her parasol.

A strange change had taken place in him since the day before—in his whole appearance, his movements, his expression. His self-confidence had disappeared and so had his serenity and his self-respect; nothing remained of his former state of mind. The recent, unforgettable impressions had blotted out all the rest. A sensation he had never experienced before took hold of him, powerful, sweet—and disturbing; a mysterious guest had entered his sanctuary, gained possession of it, and silently lay down in it at full length, like an owner in a new abode. Litvinov was no longer ashamed—he was afriad, and at the same time a desperate courage burned up within him; the vanquished, the captured are familiar with this mixture of contradictory feelings; the thief too knows something of it after his first robbery. And Litvinov had been vanquished, vanquished suddenly . . . and what had become of his honesty?

The train was several minutes late. Litvinov's

suspense turned into anguish: he could not stand still, and, pale as death, moved about jostling among the crowd. 'Good God,' he thought, 'if only I could have another twenty-four hours!...' His first glance at Tanya, her first glance at him—that was what frightened him, that was what he wanted to get over as soon as possible.... And then? And then—come what may!... He no longer made any resolutions, he no longer answered for himself. His phrase of yesterday flashed painfully through his mind.... And this was how he was meeting Tanya!

A prolonged whistle was heard at last, and heavy rumbling that increased in intensity with every minute. The railway engine appeared rolling slowly round a bend in the line. The crowd moved forward to meet it, and Litvinov followed, with dragging footsteps like one condemned. Faces, ladies' hats showed from carriage windows, a white handkerchief waved from one of them...Kapitolina Markovna was waving it...all was over: she had seen Litvinov and he recognized her. The train stopped. Litvinov rushed to the carriage door and opened it: Tatyana was standing near her aunt and holding out her hand to him with a bright smile.

He helped them both out of the carriage, said a few vague and unfinished words of welcome, and at once busied himself with their tickets, travelling bags, and rugs, ran to fetch a porter, hired a carriage; other people were bustling around him and he was glad of their presence, of the noise and the shouting. Tatyana stood a little aside and, still smiling, waited calmly for the end of his hurried arrangements. Kapitolina

Markovna, on the contrary, could not stand still: she hardly believed that she actually was at Baden after all. She suddenly called out: ' Our parasols! Tanya, where are the parasols? ' not noticing that she was holding them fast under her arm. Then she began loudly and at length saying good-bye to a lady with whom she had made friends on the way from Heidelberg to Baden. That lady was no other than our old acquaintance, Madame Suhanchikov. She had been to Heidelberg to pay homage to Gubaryov and returned with ' instructions ' from him. Kapitolina Markovna wore a rather peculiar speckled mantle and a round, mushroom-shaped travelling hat; her short white hair fell from under it in disorder. Small and thin, she was flushed from the journey and talked Russian in a piercing sing-song voice. . . . She immediately attracted attention.

Litvinov at last settled her and Tatyana in a carriage and sat down opposite to them. The horses set off. Questions were asked, handshakes renewed, smiles and words of welcome exchanged. . . . Litvinov breathed freely: the first moments passed off safely. Nothing in him, apparently, had surprised or confused Tanya: her gaze was as clear and trustful as ever, she blushed as charmingly and laughed as good-naturedly. He ventured at last to look at her, not casually and sideways, but straight and attentively: hitherto his eyes had not obeyed him. Involuntary tenderness gripped his heart: the serenity of her open, honest face was like a bitter reproach to him. ' Here, you have come, poor girl,' he thought, ' you whom I called and expected so eagerly, with whom I meant to pass the rest of my life, you've come, you've trusted me . . . and I . . . and I . . .' he bowed his head; but Kapitolina Markovna gave him no time to think: she bombarded him with questions.

'What is that building with the pillars? Where do they play roulette? Who is that going past? Tanya, Tanya, look, what crinolines! And who is that? I expect most of them here are Frenchwomen from Paris. Goodness me, what a hat! Can one find everything in the shops here, as in Paris? Oh, what an excellent, intelligent woman I've just met! You know her, Grigory Mihailitch; she told me she had met you at a Russian friend's, also remarkably clever. She promised to come and see us. The way she runs down those aristocrats is simply fine! Who is that gentleman with the grey moustache? The King of Prussia? Tanya, Tanya, look, it's the King of Prussia! No? isn't it? The Dutch ambassador? I can't hear, the wheels rattle so. Oh, what lovely trees!'

'Yes, aunt, lovely,' Tanya agreed. 'And how gay and green everything is here! Isn't it, Grigory Mihailitch?'

'Very gay,' he answered through his teeth.

The carriage stopped at last before the hotel. Litvinov accompanied both ladies to the room that had been reserved for them, promised to call in an hour's time, and returned to his room. The enchantment that had been lulled for a moment possessed him again as soon as he entered the door. There, in that room, Irina reigned since the day before; everything spoke of her, and the air itself seemed to have preserved secret traces of her presence. . . . Litvinov felt himself again to be her slave. He pulled out her handkerchief hidden on his breast, pressed his lips to it, and ardent memories spread like a subtle poison through his veins. . . . He understood that there was for him no going back, no choice; the sorrowful tenderness Tatyana had aroused in him melted like snow in the fire, and remorse died down . . . so much so that his very agitation subsided and the possibility of deception came into his mind without revolting him. . . . Love, Irina's love—that was now his truth, his law, his conscience. . . . Litvinov, always cautious and sensible, did not stop to reflect how he could escape from a situation, the horror and hideousness of which he felt but slightly and as it were from outside.

An hour had not passed when the waiter, sent by the newly arrived ladies, appeared before Litvinov: they were asking him to join them in the lounge. He followed the messenger and found them already dressed and with their hats on. Both expressed a wish to go sight-seeing at once, since the weather was lovely. Kapitolina Markovna was simply burning with impatience; she was actually vexed when she heard that it was not yet the hour for the fashionable assembly by the Konversationshaus. Litvinov offered her his arm and they set out sight-seeing. Tatyana walked by her aunt's side and looked round with calm curiosity. Kapitolina Markovna continued her questions. The sight of the roulette, of the imposing croupiers whom she certainly would have taken for Cabinet ministers had she met them elsewhere, the sight of their active little shovels, of the small heaps

159

of gold and silver on the green baize, of the gambling old ladies and painted *cocottes*, reduced Kapitolina Markovna to a kind of dumb bewilderment; she quite forgot that she ought to feel indignant, and merely gazed open-eyed, shuddering each time a new announcement was made. . . . The humming of the ivory ball in the centre of the roulette penetrated to the marrow of her bones—and only after finding herself in the fresh air again and heaving a deep sigh did she feel strong enough to call gambling an immoral invention of the aristocracy. A fixed, unpleasant smile came on to Litvinov's lips; he spoke abruptly and lazily, as though he were bored or vexed. . . . But when he turned to Tatyana he was secretly abashed: she was looking at him attentively and with an expression as though she were asking herself what exactly she thought of him. He hastened to nod to her, she nodded back to him, and again she looked at him questioningly with some effort as though he were much further away from her than he really was. Litvinov took his ladies away from the Konversationshaus, and passing by the 'Russian tree,' under which some of their fellow countrywomen were already settled, led them towards Lichtenthal. They had no sooner reached the avenue than he saw Irina in the distance.

She was walking towards them with her husband and Potugin. Litvinov turned white as a sheet but did not slow down his pace and, on meeting her, bowed in silence. She too bowed to him amiably but coldly and, rapidly scanning Tatyana, glided past. . . . Ratmirov raised his hat, Potugin muttered something.

' Who is that lady? ' Tatyana asked suddenly. She had scarcely opened her lips until that moment.

' That lady? ' Litvinov repeated. ' That lady? A certain Madame Ratmirov.'

' Russian? '

' Yes.'

' Have you got to know her here? '

' No; I knew her before.'

' How beautiful she is ! '

' Have you noticed her dress? ' Kapitolina Markovna intervened. ' Ten families could have been kept for a whole year on the price of her lace alone. Was that her husband with her? ' she asked Litvinov.

' Yes, her husband.'

' He must be awfully rich? '

' I really don't know; I don't think so.'

' And what is his rank? '

' He is a general.'

' What eyes she has ! ' Tatyana remarked, ' and such a strange expression in them: both dreamy and penetrating. . . . I've never seen such eyes.'

Litvinov made no answer; he fancied he again felt on his face Tatyana's questioning look, but he was mistaken: she was looking at the sandy path under her feet.

' Good heavens ! Who is that scarecrow? ' Kapitolina Markovna exclaimed suddenly, pointing to a low carriage in which a red-haired, snub-nosed woman in extremely luxurious attire and lilac stockings was lolling impudently.

' That scarecrow! Why, that 's the famous Mam'zelle Corá.'

161

' Who? '

' Mam'zelle Corá . . . a Paris . . . celebrity.'

' What? That pug? But she is hideous? '

'Evidently that's no obstacle.'

Kapitolina Markovna merely threw up her hands.

' Well, your Baden is a place ! ' she uttered at last. 'And may one sit down on the seat here? I'm rather tired.'

' Of course you may, Kapitolina Markovna. . . . That's what garden seats are for.'

' But there's no telling ! They say in Paris there are also seats on the boulevards, but it's improper to sit down there.'

Litvinov made no answer; he grasped only at that moment that the place where he had his decisive interview with Irina was only two steps away. Then he recalled that he had just noticed a small rosy mark on her cheek. . . .

Kapitolina Markovna sank down on to the seat; Tatyana settled next to her. Litvinov remained standing; something was happening—or was it only his fancy?—between him and Tatyana . . . gradually and unconsciously.

' Ah, the silly monkey ! ' said Kapitolina Markovna, compassionately shaking her head. ' Why, the cost of *her* clothes would keep not ten but a hundred families. Did you notice the diamonds in her red hair under her hat? Diamonds in the day-time, what do you think of that, eh? '

' Her hair isn't red,' Litvinov remarked, 'she dyes it red, it's the fashion now.'

Kapitolina Markovna threw up her hands again;

162

she was actually reduced to silence. 'Well,' she said at last, 'with us in Dresden there's nothing so scandalous. It's further away from Paris, that's why. Don't you think so, Grigory Mihailitch?'

'I?' Litvinov answered while he asked himself, 'What is she talking about?' 'I? certainly. . . . Of course.'

At that moment there was a sound of unhurried footsteps, and Potugin came up to the seat.

'How do you do, Grigory Mihailitch?' he said, smiling and nodding.

Litvinov seized him by the hand at once.

'How do you do, how do you do, Sozont Ivanitch? I believe I've just met you with . . . just now, in the avenue.'

'Yes, it was me.'

Potugin bowed respectfully to the two ladies.

'Allow me to introduce you, Sozont Ivanitch. My old friends and relatives who have just arrived at Baden; Potugin, Sozont Ivanitch, our fellow countryman, also a visitor at Baden.'

Both ladies rose slightly from the seat. Potugin bowed again.

'It's a regular *réunion* here,' Kapitolina Markovna began in a high-pitched voice; the kind old lady was very shy, but tried at all costs to keep up her dignity. 'Every one considers it a pleasant duty to visit Baden.'

'Baden certainly is a very pleasant place,' Potugin answered glancing sideways at Tatyana, 'very pleasant.'

'Yes; but much too fashionable, so far as I can judge. She and I have been living in Dresden all this time . . . a very interesting town; but here it really is like a *réunion*.'

' She's taken a fancy to the word,' Potugin thought. 'That's a very true remark,' he said aloud, 'but it's a beautiful spot and the scenery is hard to beat. Your companion especially will be sure to appreciate it. Isn't it so, madam? ' he added addressing Tatyana directly.

Tatyana raised her large clear eyes to Potugin. She seemed to wonder what was wanted of her and why Litvinov introduced her on the very first day of her arrival to this stranger, though he had a good and intelligent face and was looking at her with a kind and friendly expression.

' Yes,' she said at last, ' it's very nice here.'

' You must see the Old Castle,' Potugin continued, ' and I specially advise you to go to Iburg.'

'The Saxon Switzerland——' Kapitolina Markovna began. A blast of trumpets resounded down the avenue: that was the Prussian military band from Rastadt (in 1862 Rastadt was still an allied fortress) beginning their weekly concert at the pavilion. Kapitolina Markovna got up at once.

' Music! ' she said. 'Music *à la Conversation*! We must go there. It is past three o'clock now, isn't it? Is it the time when society gathers? '

' Yes,' Potugin answered, 'it's the most fashionable hour and the music is excellent.'

' Well, then there's no time to waste. Come, Tanya.'

' Will you allow me to accompany you? ' Potugin asked to Litvinov's considerable surprise: it never

entered his head that Potugin had been sent by
Irina.

Kapitolina Markovna smiled politely.

'With the greatest pleasure, M'sieur—M'sieur——'

'Potugin,' he prompted her and offered her his
arm. Litvinov offered his to Tatyana and both pairs
walked towards the Konversationshaus.

Potugin went on talking to Kapitolina Markovna.
But Litvinov walked without saying a word, and only,
once or twice, smiled without any reason and slightly
pressed Tatyana's arm. There was falsity in those
contacts, to which she did not respond, and Litvinov
was aware of the falsity. They were no longer, as in
the old days, a mutual confirmation of the close union
of two hearts devoted to each other, but merely replaced, for the time being, words which he could
not find. The something unspoken that had begun
between them grew and gained strength. Tatyana
again looked at him attentively, almost intently.

The same thing went on when the four of them sat
down at a small table by the Konversationshaus, the
only difference being that Litvinov's silence seemed
more natural in the noise and bustle of the crowd
and the clash and thunder of the music. Kapitolina
Markovna was at the height of excitement; Potugin
scarcely had time to reply to her and to satisfy her
curiosity. Fortunately for him there suddenly appeared
in the crowd the thin figure of Madame Suhanchikov
with her glittering restless eyes. Kapitolina Markovna
recognized her at once, called to her, made her sit
down at their table—and a regular storm of words
broke out.

Potugin turned to Tatyana and began talking to her in a soft, gentle voice, with a friendly expression in his face as he slightly bent down to her; and she, to her own surprise, answered him freely and easily. She enjoyed talking to this unknown man, a complete stranger to her, while Litvinov sat still as before, with the same fixed and unpleasant smile on his lips.

It was dinner time at last. The music stopped, the crowd grew thinner. Kapitolina Markovna took a friendly leave of Madame Suhanchikov. She had conceived a great respect for her, though she confessed to her niece afterwards that the lady was much too embittered—but she did know everything about every one! And they certainly ought to get the sewing machines as soon as the wedding was over.

Potugin said good-bye; Litvinov took his ladies home. At the hotel entrance a letter was handed to him; he stepped aside and hastily tore open the envelope. The following words were written in pencil on a small piece of vellum paper: 'Come to me at seven o'clock to-night for a minute, I implore you. Irina.' Litvinov thrust the paper into his pocket and, turning round, smiled again—at whom? what for? Tatyana was standing with her back to him.

Dinner was served at the common table at the hotel. Litvinov sat between Kapitolina Markovna and Tatyana and, suddenly possessed by a strange animation, talked, told anecdotes, poured out wine for himself and the ladies. He behaved so exuberantly that a French infantry officer from Strasburg with an 'imperial' and moustache à la Napoleon III, sitting opposite to him, felt at liberty to take part in the conversation and actually ended by proposing a toast *à la santé des belles Moscovites*! When the dinner was over Litvinov conducted the ladies to their room, and after standing in silence by the window for a few minutes with a gloomy expression, suddenly declared that he must leave them for a short time on business, but would be sure to return before the evening.

Tatyana said nothing, but she turned pale and lowered her eyes. Kapitolina Markovna had the habit of sleeping after dinner; Tatyana knew that Litvinov was aware of this and had hoped that he would take advantage of the opportunity and stay, for he had not been alone with her since their arrival, had not spoken to her frankly. And here he was going out! What was she to make of it? What did it mean? And indeed his whole behaviour during the day——

Litvinov hastened away without waiting for objections. Kapitolina Markovna lay down on the sofa, and after a few sighs and murmurs sank into untroubled sleep. Tatyana went to a corner of the room and sat down in a low chair, tightly folding her arms on her breast.

XIX

LITVINOV walked quickly up the stairs of the Hôtel de l'Europe. A little girl of about thirteen, with a sly Calmuck face, who had evidently been on the look-out for him, stopped him and said: 'This way, please. Irina Pavlovna will not be long.' He looked at her in perplexity. She smiled, repeated 'This way, please,' and led him into a small room facing Irina's bedroom and filled with trunks and boxes. The little girl disappeared, shutting the door quietly. Litvinov had scarcely had time to look round when the door opened again and Irina appeared in a pink evening dress, with pearls round her neck and in her hair. She rushed towards him, seized both his hands, and remained silent for a few moments; her eyes were shining and her breast heaving as though she had been running uphill.

'I could not receive you . . . there,' she began in a hurried whisper, 'we are just going to a dinner party, but I was determined to see you. . . . It was your betrothed, wasn't it, with whom I met you to-day?'

'Yes it was my betrothed,' Litvinov answered, stressing the word 'was.'

'Well, and so I wanted to see you for a minute just to tell you that you must consider yourself perfectly free, that what happened yesterday must not change your plans in the least. . . .'

'Irina!' Litvinov cried. 'Why do you say this?'

He said these words in a loud voice . . . they rang with unbounded passion. Irina involuntarily closed her eyes for a moment.

'Oh, my dearest,' she went on in a still softer whisper than before, but with irrepressible eagerness, 'you don't know how I love you. . . . Yesterday I merely paid my debt, made up for my guilt in the past. . . . Oh! I could not give you my youth as I would, but I haven't laid any obligations upon you, I haven't absolved you from any other promise, my dear one! Do what you like, you are free as air, you aren't bound in any way, I want you to know it!'

'But I can't live without you, Irina,' Litvinov interrupted her also in a whisper. 'Since yesterday I am yours for ever. . . . It's only at your feet that I can breathe. . . .'

Tremulously he bent over her hands. Irina looked down on his bowed head.

'Well, know then,' she said, 'that I too am ready for anything, that I too will consider no one and nothing. It shall be as you decide. I too am for ever yours . . . yours.'

Someone cautiously rapped at the door. Irina bent down, whispered once more, 'I am yours . . . good-bye.' Litvinov felt her breath on his hair, the touch of her lips. When he drew himself up she was no longer in the room; only her dress rustled in the passage, and in the distance Ratmirov's voice said: '*Eh bien? Vous ne venez pas?*'

Litvinov sat down on a big trunk and covered his face with his hands. He breathed in a feminine

169

fragrance, subtle and fresh . . . Irina had held his hands in hers. 'It's too much—too much,' he thought.

The little girl came into the room and said, smiling again in answer to his anxious look:

'Please come away now.'

He got up and went out of the hotel. It was out of the question to go straight home: he had to recover. His heart was beating heavily and unevenly; the ground seemed to sway under his feet. Litvinov again walked down the Lichtenthal Avenue. He understood that the decisive moment was at hand, that it was impossible to put things off, to hide and turn away, that an explanation with Tatyana was inevitable. He pictured to himself how she sat there without moving and waited for him . . . he foresaw what he would say to her, but how was he to begin, how was he to set about it? He had dismissed without a thought all his reasonable, well-ordered, respectable future: he knew that he was flinging himself headlong into a whirlpool which was not safe even to look at . . . but it was not this that troubled him. That was settled and done with, but how was he to appear before his judge? And if he really were to meet a judge—an angel with a flaming sword—it would be easier for the guilty heart . . . but it was he himself who would have to plunge the knife in. . . . Hideous! But to go back, to renounce the other, to take advantage of the freedom that was promised to him and recognized as his due. . . . No, he'd rather die! No, he didn't want that hateful freedom . . . but he'd gladly sink into the dust if only those eyes would look down with love. . . .

'Grigory Mihailitch!' said a sad voice, and some-
body's hand was laid heavily on Litvinov's shoulder.
He turned round in some alarm and recognized
Potugin.

'Excuse me, Grigory Mihailitch,' he began with
his usual constraint, 'I may have disturbed you, but
seeing you from a distance, I thought—— But if you
don't want me——'

'On the contrary, I'm very pleased,' Litvinov said
through his teeth.

Potugin walked beside him.

'It's a beautiful evening,' he began, 'so warm!
Have you been out long?'

'No, not long.'

'But indeed I needn't ask; I saw you leave the
Hôtel de l'Europe.'

'Were you following me?'

'Yes.'

'Have you something to say to me?'

'Yes,' Potugin repeated almost inaudibly. Litvinov stopped and looked at his uninvited companion.
His face was pale, his eyes wandered; the old sorrow
of long ago seemed to have come to the surface in his
distorted features.

'What is it exactly you want to tell me?' Litvinov
said slowly and moved forward again.

'I'll tell you in a minute—if you'll allow me.
If you don't mind, let's sit down on this seat here.
It will be more convenient.'

'Why, this is something mysterious,' Litvinov said,
sitting down beside him. 'You don't seem to be
quite yourself, Sozont Ivanitch.'

171

'No, I'm all right, and there's nothing mysterious either. I wanted to tell you . . . the impression that your betrothed made on me—she is your betrothed, isn't she?—well, I mean the young lady to whom you've introduced me to-day. I must say I haven't in all my life met a more lovable creature. She has a heart of gold, a truly angelic spirit.'

Potugin uttered these words with the same bitter and sorrowful expression, so that even Litvinov could not help noticing the strange contradiction between what he said and the expression with which he said it.

'You are quite right in what you say about Tatyana Petrovna,' Litvinov began, 'though I am bound to say I am surprised both at your knowing what my relation to her is and at your understanding her so quickly. She really has an angelic nature; but may I ask, is this the subject you wished to discuss with me?'

'One cannot help understanding her,' Potugin continued as though avoiding the last question. 'It's enough to look into her eyes. She deserves all possible happiness, and the man whose lot it is to give her this happiness is indeed to be envied! One must only wish that he may prove worthy of his lot.'

Litvinov frowned slightly.

'Excuse me, Sozont Ivanitch,' he brought out, 'I confess I find our conversation rather peculiar. I should like to know, does the hint contained in your words refer to me?'

Potugin did not answer Litvinov at once; he was evidently struggling with himself.

'Grigory Mihailitch,' he began at last, 'either I am completely mistaken in you, or you are capable of hearing the truth from whomsoever it may come and in however unattractive a guise. I said to you just now that I saw where you came from.'

' Well, yes, from the Hôtel de l'Europe. What of it?'

' But I know whom you met there.'

' How do you mean?'

' You met Madame Ratmirov.'

' Well, yes, I've been to see her. What then?'

' What then? . . . You who are betrothed to Tatyana Petrovna have been to Madame Ratmirov whom you love—and who loves you.'

Litvinov instantly jumped up from the seat; the blood rushed to his head.

' What is this,' he brought out at last in an angry, stifled voice, 'a silly joke? Spying? Explain yourself, please.'

Potugin cast a melancholy glance on him.

'Ah, don't be offended at my words, Grigory Mihailitch—nothing that you may say can offend me. It wasn't for that I spoke to you, and I am in no mood for joking.'

' Perhaps, perhaps. I am ready to believe in the purity of your intentions, but I must ask you, all the same, what right have you to interfere with another man's private affairs and intimate life, and on what grounds do you assert so self-confidently that . . . your invention is true?'

' My invention! Had I invented it you wouldn't have been angry! And as for my right, I've never heard that a man should ask himself whether he had a right to hold out a hand to one who is drowning.'

' Thank you very much for your solicitude,'

Litvinov caught him up wrathfully, ' but I don't need it in the least, and I regard all those phrases about the snares set by society ladies for inexperienced young men, the immorality of the smart set and so on, as mere phrases, and in a sense despise them, and so I beg you to spare your rescuing arm, and let me drown in peace.'

Potugin once more raised his eyes to Litvinov. He breathed unevenly and his lips twitched.

' But look at me, young man,' broke out from him at last and he rapped himself on the chest, ' do I look like an ordinary complacent moralist or preacher? Don't you understand that out of mere sympathy for you, however strong it might be, I wouldn't have uttered a word or given you a right to accuse me of what I hate above all—intrusiveness? Don't you see that it's something utterly different, that you have before you a man broken, shattered, destroyed by that very feeling from the consequences of which he would like to save you—and for the same woman!'

Litvinov stepped back.

'Is it possible! What did you say? You—you— Sozont Ivanitch? But Madame Belsky — that child——'

' Oh, don't question me—believe me! That was a dark, terrible story which I will not tell you. I scarcely knew Madame Belsky—that child is not mine, I took it all upon myself because *she* wanted it. Why else do you suppose I should be here, in your horrid Baden? And besides, do you suppose, could you imagine for a minute that I'd have ventured to warn you simply out of pity for you? I am sorry for that good, sweet girl, your betrothed, but after all what do I care for your future and for both of you? . . . No, it's for her I am afraid . . . for her!'

'You do me much honour, Mr. Potugin,' Litvinov began, 'but since, according to you, we are both in the same position, why don't you read the same admonitions to yourself? And aren't your fears due to another feeling?'

'You mean, to jealousy? Ah, young man, you should be ashamed to dissemble and prevaricate—ashamed not to understand what bitter sorrow makes me speak! No, we are not in the same position! I—I'm a perfectly harmless eccentric old creature, and you—— But what's the good of talking! You wouldn't agree for a moment to play the part I play—and play with gratitude, too! Jealousy! Those who haven't a grain of hope aren't jealous, and this wouldn't have been the first occasion for me to experience that feeling. It's only that I'm afraid—afraid for her, do understand that. How could I have expected, when you sent me for you, that the sense of guilt to which she confessed would carry her so far?'

'But excuse me, Sozont Ivanitch, you seem to know——'

'I know nothing, and I know everything. I know,' he added, turning his head away, 'I know where she was yesterday. But there's no holding her back now: like a stone that's been thrown, she must roll to the bottom. It would be even more foolish of me to imagine that my words would hold you back at once . . . you, to whom such a woman. . . . But enough of that. I couldn't control myself, that's my excuse. And besides, how is one

to know, and why not try? Perhaps you'll bethink
yourself, perhaps something I've said will sink into
your mind and you will not wish to ruin her and
yourself and that beautiful innocent creature. . . . Ah,
don't be angry, don't stamp! What have I to fear?
Why should I stand on ceremony? It's not jealousy
speaking in me now, not vexation. . . . I'm ready to
fall at your feet, to implore you. . . . But good-bye.
Don't be afraid, it shall all remain a secret. I wished
for your good.'

Potugin walked away down the avenue and soon
disappeared in the gathering darkness. . . . Litvinov
did not detain him.

'A dark, terrible story . . .' Potugin had said to
Litvinov and would not tell it. . . . Let us, too, touch
upon it in a few words only.

Some eight years before, Potugin was sent by his
Ministry to do some temporary work for Count
Reisenbach. It was in the summer. Potugin used
to go to the count's summer residence with the papers
and spent whole days there. Irina at that time was
living at the count's. She never despised people in
a humble station in life, at any rate never avoided
them, and the countess more than once found fault
with her for her excessive Moscow familiarity. Irina
soon detected an intelligent man in the modest government clerk buttoned up to the chin in his official
uniform. She talked to him often and with pleasure
. . . and he . . . he fell in love with her passionately,
deeply, secretly. . . . Secretly! *He* thought so. The
summer passed; the count no longer needed an extra
assistant. Potugin lost sight of Irina, but he could

not forget her. Some three years later he quite
unexpectedly received an invitation from a certain
lady of the middle class whom he scarcely knew.
The lady was at first slightly embarrassed at explaining
her business, but having made him promise on his
oath to keep strictly secret all that he was going to
hear, offered him . . . a marriage with a young lady
who occupied a prominent position in society and for
whom marriage had become a necessity. The lady
scarcely ventured to hint at the chief person concerned
and then offered Potugin money—a great deal of
money. Potugin was not offended—he was too
much surprised to be angry — but, of course, he
refused point-blank. Then the lady gave him a
note—from Irina. ' You are a good and noble
man,' she wrote, ' and I know you would do anything
for me; I beg you for this sacrifice. You will save
one who is very dear to me. In saving her, you will
save me too.... Don't ask how. I would not have
ventured to turn to any.one with such a request, but
to you I hold out my hands and say: do it for my
sake.' Potugin pondered and said that he certainly
was ready to do a great deal for Irina Pavlovna, but
he would like to hear her wish from her own lips.
The meeting took place that same evening: it did
not last long, and no one knew about it except
that lady. Irina was no longer living at Count
Reisenbach's.
    ' Why did you think of me of all people? ' Potugin
asked her. She began talking about his excellent
qualities, but suddenly pulled herself up.
    ' No,' she said, ' with you one must speak the

177

truth. I knew, I know that you love me: that's why I ventured . . . ' and she told him the whole story.

Elise Belsky was an orphan; her relatives were not fond of her and reckoned on her inheritance . . . she was faced with ruin. In saving her, Irina really was doing a service to him who was at the bottom of it all and who now stood in a very close relation to Irina herself.

Potugin gave Irina a long, silent look and agreed. She wept and, all in tears, fell on his neck. He, too, wept . . . but their tears were very different. Everything was being prepared for a secret marriage, a powerful hand removed all obstacles. . . . But illness came . . . then a daughter was born, and then the mother—poisoned herself. What was to be done with the child? Potugin received it into his care from the same hands—the hands of Irina.

A terrible, dark story. . . . Pass it by, reader, pass it by!

More than an hour had passed before Litvinov made up his mind to return to his hotel. He was nearing it when he heard footsteps behind him. Somebody seemed to be following him doggedly and to be hastening his steps when Litvinov walked faster. Coming up to a lamp-post Litvinov turned round and recognized General Ratmirov. Wearing a white tie and a number of stars and crosses on a gold chain in the buttonhole of his dress-coat, his smart overcoat flung open, the general was returning from the dinner party, alone. His eyes insolently fixed on Litvinov expressed such hatred and contempt, his whole figure suggested such aggressive defiance, that Litvinov felt it his duty to go to meet him and, very reluctantly, face 'a scandal.' But when they were on a level the general's face changed instantly: it assumed its usual look of playful elegance, and his hand in a light lilac glove raised his polished hat high above his head. Litvinov took his hat off in silence, and each went his own way.

'He must have noticed something,' Litvinov thought.

'If at least it were . . . someone else,' thought the general.

Tatyana and her aunt were playing piquet when Litvinov entered their room.

'Well, you're a fine one, my dear!' Kapitolina Markovna exclaimed, throwing down the cards. 'The very first day, and you've been gone the whole evening! We've been waiting and waiting and scolding you. . . .'

'I said nothing, aunt,' Tatyana remarked.

'Oh, we all know you're a meek one! For shame, sir! and to think you are betrothed!'

Litvinov apologized as best he could and sat down to the table.

'Why have you left off playing?' he asked after a pause.

'What next! We play cards from boredom, when there's nothing to do . . . and now you've come.'

'If you'd like to listen to the evening music,' Litvinov said, 'I'll be delighted to come with you.'

Kapitolina Markovna looked at her niece.

'Let's go, aunt,' Tatyana said, 'I am ready—but wouldn't it be better to stay at home?'

'Yes, certainly! Let's have tea in our Moscow

way, with a samovar, and let's have a good chat. We haven't had any real talk yet.'

Litvinov ordered tea, but they did not succeed in having a good chat. He was feeling continual remorse; whatever he said, he fancied that he was telling lies and that Tatyana saw through it. And yet there was no change to be noticed in her; her manner was as free from constraint as usual . . . only her eyes never dwelt on Litvinov, but glided over him with a kind of timorous indulgence—and she was paler than usual. Kapitolina Markovna asked her if she had a headache.

Tatyana was on the point of answering no, but after a moment's thought she said, ' Yes, a slight one.'

' It's the journey,' Litvinov remarked, and he actually blushed with shame.

' Yes, the journey,' Tatyana repeated, and again her glance glided over him.

' You should have a rest, dear.'

' Yes, I'll soon go to bed, aunt.'

A copy of the *Guide des Voyageurs* lay on the table; Litvinov began reading aloud the description of places around Baden.

' That's all very well,' Kapitolina Markovna interrupted him, ' but there's one thing we mustn't forget. They say linen is very cheap here, so we'd better buy some for your future home.'

Tatyana lowered her eyes.

' There'll be plenty of time for that, aunt. You never think of yourself, but you certainly ought to have a new dress. You see how smart every one is here.'

180

' Eh, my dear, what ever for? Smartness is not in my line. It would be different if I were such a beauty as that friend of yours, Grigory Mihailitch, what's her name?'

' Which friend?'

' The one whom we met to-day.'

' Ah, that one!' Litvinov said with assumed indifference, and again he felt disgusted and ashamed. ' No,' he thought, ' I can't go on like this.'

He was sitting next to his betrothed, and at a few inches' distance from her in his side pocket lay Irina's handkerchief.

Kapitolina Markovna went for a minute into the next room. ' Tanya. . .' Litvinov brought out with an effort. It was the first time he called her by her pet name that day.

She turned to him.

' I—I have something important to tell you.'

' Ah! Indeed? When? Now?'

' No, to-morrow.'

' Ah! to-morrow. Very well.'

Infinite pity flooded Litvinov's heart. He took Tatyana's hand and kissed it humbly, like one at fault; she felt a slight pang at her breast, and the kiss brought her no joy.

After one o'clock in the morning Kapitolina Markovna, who slept in the same room with her niece, suddenly raised her head and listened.

' Tanya!' she said, ' are you crying?'

Tatyana did not answer at once.

' No, aunt,' her gentle voice was heard, ' I have a cold.'

181

XX

'Why did I say it to her?' Litvinov thought the next morning as he sat before the window in his room. He shrugged his shoulders with vexation: he had said it to Tatyana precisely because he wanted to cut off all way of retreat for himself. A note from Irina lay in the window: she was asking him to come at twelve o'clock. Potugin's words continually came into his mind; they were like a sinister but faint subterranean roar; he was angry and could not get rid of them. Someone knocked at his door.

'*Wer da?*' Litvinov asked.

'Ah! you're at home! Open!' said Bindasov's hoarse bass.

The door handle creaked.

Litvinov turned pale with anger.

'I am not at home,' he said sharply.

'How not at home? What trick is this now?'

'I tell you I'm not at home: clear out.'

'That's a nice thing! And I've come to borrow some money,' Bindasov grumbled.

He went away, however, stamping as usual.

Litvinov very nearly ran after him: he felt sorely tempted to kick the hateful bully downstairs. The happenings of the last few days had upset his nerves: a little more and he would have burst into tears. He drank a glass of cold water, locked all the drawers, not knowing why he did it, and went to Tatyana.

He found her alone. Kapitolina Markovna had gone out shopping. Tatyana sat on the sofa holding a book in both hands: she was not reading it and indeed scarcely knew what book it was. She did not move, but her heart was beating violently and the white collar round her neck quivered visibly at regular intervals.

Litvinov was confused ... but he sat down beside her, said 'Good morning,' smiled; and she smiled at him too without speaking. She bowed to him when he came in, politely as to a stranger—and did not look at him. He held out his hand to her; she gave him her cold fingers, but disengaged them at once and took hold of the book again. Litvinov felt that it would be an insult to Tatyana to begin talking of insignificant things; as usual she was not making any demands, but everything in her said, 'I'm waiting, I'm waiting.' He had to fulfil his promise. But—although he had spent most of the night thinking about it—he had not prepared even the first introductory words, and did not know in the least how to break the cruel silence.

'Tanya,' he began at last, 'I told you yesterday that I have something of importance to tell you. I am ready, only I beg you beforehand not to be angry with me, and to believe that my feelings for you——'

He stopped. His breath failed him. Tatyana did not stir or look at him: she merely clutched her book more tightly.

'We have always been ...' Litvinov continued,

not having finished the sentence, 'we have always been perfectly frank with each other; I respect you too deeply to prevaricate with you; I want to prove to you that I value your lofty and independent nature, and although I . . . although, of course——'

'Grigory Mihailitch,' Tatyana began in an even voice, and a deadly pallor overspread her face, 'I'll come to your aid: you no longer love me and you don't know how to tell me so.'

Litvinov gave an involuntary start.

'But why?' he brought out almost inaudibly. 'What led you to think that?. . . I really don't understand. . . .'

'Well, isn't it true? Isn't it true, tell me? Tell me!' Tatyana turned round to Litvinov; her face, with her hair drawn back from it, drew close to his, and her eyes that had so long avoided him looked intently into his eyes.

'Isn't it true?' she repeated.

He said nothing, he did not utter a sound. He could not have lied at that moment even if he had known that she would believe him and that his lie would save her; he could not even meet her eyes. He said nothing, but she no longer needed an answer; she had read that answer in his very silence, in his guilty, downcast eyes—she leaned back and dropped the book. . . . Up to that moment she had still doubted, and Litvinov understood this; he understood that she had still been uncertain—and how hideous, how really hideous was all that he had done!

He sank on his knees before her.

'Tanya!' he exclaimed, 'if you only knew how

184

wretched I am to see you in this position, how dreadful it is to think that it is my—my doing! My heart is torn to pieces; I don't recognize myself; I have lost myself, and you, and everything. . . . All, all is ruined, Tanya! Could I expect that I . . . I should deal such a blow to you, my best friend, my guardian angel! . . . Could I expect that this is how we should meet, should spend such a day as yesterday!'

Tatyana was about to get up and go. He held her back by the border of her dress.

'No, listen to me for another minute. You see, I'm on my knees before you, but I haven't come to ask your forgiveness—you cannot and must not forgive me—I've come to tell you that your friend is lost, that he's falling into an abyss and doesn't want to drag you with him. . . . And to save me . . . no! not even you can save me. I'd be the first to push you away. . . . I'm lost, Tanya, I'm lost utterly!'

Tatyana looked at Litvinov.

'You're lost!' she repeated as though not quite understanding. 'You're lost?'

'Yes, Tanya, I'm lost. All my past, all that I loved, all by which I've lived—is lost to me; all is shattered, all is ruined, and I don't know what lies before me. You've said just now that I no longer loved you. . . . No, Tanya, it isn't that, but another, terrible, irresistible feeling has come upon me like a torrent. . . . I fought against it as long as I could. . . .'

Tatyana stood up; her brows contracted in a frown; her pale face was darkened. Litvinov stood up too.

'You've fallen in love with another woman,' she began, 'and I guess who she is. . . . We met her yesterday, didn't we? Well, I know what there's left for me to do. Since you say yourself that this feeling in you is unalterable—' Tatyana paused for a second; perhaps she still hoped that Litvinov would not let that last word pass without protest, but he said nothing—'it remains to me to return to you . . . your word.'

Litvinov bowed his head as though submissively receiving a blow he had deserved.

'You have a right to be indignant with me,' he said. 'You have every right to reproach me for cowardice . . . for deceit.'

Tatyana looked at him again.

'I haven't reproached you, Litvinov, I don't accuse you. I agree with you: the most bitter truth is better than what happened yesterday. What sort of a life would ours have been now?'

'What sort of a life will mine be now?' echoed mournfully in Litvinov's mind.

Tatyana went up to the bedroom door.

'I beg you to leave me alone for a time, Grigory Mihailitch—we shall see each other again, we'll have a talk. All this was so sudden. I must pull myself together . . . leave me . . . spare my pride. We'll meet again.'

With these words Tatyana quickly withdrew and locked herself in.

Litvinov came out into the street like one dazed or stunned; something dark and heavy settled in the very depths of his heart; a similar sensation must be felt by a man who has cut another's throat; but at the same time he felt at ease as though he had thrown off at

SMOKE

last some hateful burden. Tatyana's magnanimity
crushed him, he was keenly conscious of all that he
was losing ... and yet his repentance was mixed
with annoyance; he was longing to go to Irina as the
only refuge that was left him—and at the same time
he was angry with her. For the last few days Litvinov's feelings had been growing more and more
intense and confused; this confusion tormented,
exasperated him, he felt lost in it. All he was thirsting
for was to come out at last on to a path, whatever it
might be, so that he need not circle round and round
in this incomprehensible twilight. Practical people
like Litvinov ought not to be carried away by passion;
it destroys the very meaning of their life. . . . But
nature takes no account of logic, of our human logic;
she has one of her own, which we do not understand
or acknowledge till we are crushed under its
wheel.

After parting from Tatyana Litvinov had only one
thing in mind: to see Irina; and he went to her. But
the general was at home—at any rate, so the hall-porter
told him—and he did not like to go in, he did not feel
equal to keeping up appearances. He dragged himself to the Konversationshaus. Both Voroshilov and
Pishchalkin, whom Litvinov happened to meet, suffered
from his inability to pretend that day: he blurted out to
the one that he was empty as a drum and to the other
that he bored one to extinction. It was a good thing
Bindasov had not turned up: there would certainly
have been a ' *grosser Scandal.*' Both the young men
were surprised: Voroshilov actually asked himself
whether his honour as an officer demanded satisfaction

187

—but, like Gogol's lieutenant Pirogov, comforted himself with sandwiches in a café.

Litvinov saw from a distance Kapitolina Markovna who was busily running in her striped mantle from shop to shop. . . . He was conscience-stricken at the sight of the kind, absurd, noble-hearted old lady. Then he recalled Potugin and their conversation of the day before. . . . Suddenly something intangible and unmistakable was wafted to him; the breath of a falling shadow could not be more elusive, but he felt at once that it was Irina drawing near. And indeed she appeared a few paces away from him, arm in arm with another lady; their eyes met at once. Irina must have noticed something peculiar in Litvinov's expression; she stopped in front of a shop window full of tiny wooden clocks of Black Forest make and beckoned to him with a motion of her head. She pointed out to him one of those pretty clocks with a coloured cuckoo at the top, and, while inviting him to admire it, she said, not in a whisper but in her ordinary voice, as though continuing a sentence she had begun—that is less likely to attract other people's attention:

' Come in an hour's time, I shall be at home alone.'

But at that moment the ' ladies' man ' Monsieur Verdier dashed up to her and went into raptures over the *feuille-morte* colour of her dress and her low-crowned Spanish hat tilted almost over her eyebrows. . . . Litvinov disappeared in the crowd.

XXI

'GRIGORY,' Irina said to him two hours later, sitting next to him on the sofa and resting both her hands on his shoulders, 'what's the matter with you? Tell me now, quick, while we are alone.'

'With me?' Litvinov answered. 'I am happy, happy, that's what's the matter with me.'

Irina lowered her eyes, smiled, and sighed.

'That's not an answer to my question, darling.'

Litvinov pondered.

'Well then, let me tell you, since you insist upon knowing' (Irina opened her eyes wide and drew slightly back), 'I've told everything to my betrothed to-day.'

'How, everything? You told her my name?'

Litvinov threw up his hands in dismay.

'For goodness' sake, Irina, how could you imagine such a thing! as though I could——'

'There, forgive...forgive me. What then have you said to her?'

'I told her that I loved her no more.'

'Has she asked why?'

'I didn't conceal from her that I loved another, and that she and I must part.'

'Well...and what did she say? Did she agree?'

'Oh, Irina! what a girl she is! She is the soul of generosity and self-sacrifice!'

'I well believe it ... though indeed she had no choice in the matter.'

'And not a word of reproach, not a word of bitterness to me, who have ruined her whole life, deceived her, pitilessly thrown her over. . . .'

Irina was examining her finger-nails.

'Tell me, Grigory ... did she love you?'

'Yes, Irina, she loved me.'

Irina paused and straightened her dress.

'I must say,' she began, 'I don't quite understand why you suddenly decided to have it out with her.'

'Why? But surely you wouldn't have me tell lies and pretend to her, to one so pure in heart? Or did you suppose——'

'I didn't suppose anything,' Irina interrupted. 'I confess I haven't given her much thought. . . . I am no good at thinking of two people at once.'

'That is, you mean to say——'

'Well, what then? Is she going away, that pure heart?' Irina interrupted him again.

'I know nothing,' Litvinov answered. 'I have to see her again. But she won't stay.'

'Ah! A pleasant journey!'

'No, she won't stay. Though I, too, am not thinking of her now, I am thinking of what *you* said, of what *you* promised me.'

Irina looked at him from under her brows.

'You ungrateful man! Aren't you content yet?'

'No, Irina, I'm not content. You've made me happy, but I am not content, and you understand me.'

'That is, I——'

'Yes, you understand me. Recall your words,

recall what you wrote me. I cannot share you with another. No, no, I can't agree to play the miserable part of a secret lover. I've thrown not only my own life, but another life too, at your feet, I've given up everything, I've shattered everything to fragments, irretrievably and without regret—but I believe, I'm firmly convinced that you too will keep your promise and unite your lot with mine for ever....'

'You want me to run away with you? I am ready—'Litvinov ecstatically covered her hands with kisses—'I am ready, I am not going back on my words. But have you considered all the difficulties ...prepared the means?'

'I? I haven't had time to think over or prepare anything, but only say yes, only let me act, and in less than a month——'

'A month! We are going to Italy in a fortnight.'

'A fortnight is enough for me. Oh, Irina, you seem to treat my proposal coldly, perhaps you think it fantastic, but I'm not a boy, I'm not used to playing with dreams, I know what a terrible step it is, I know what a responsibility I'm taking upon myself—but I see no other way out. And, besides, I must break all ties with the past if only not to appear a contemptible liar in the eyes of the girl I have sacrificed to you!'

Irina drew herself up suddenly and her eyes blazed.

'There you must excuse me, Grigory Mihailitch! If I make up my mind, if I do run away, I'll run away with a man who'll do it for my sake, my sake alone, and not so as not to lower himself in the opinion of a phlegmatic young lady with milk and water, *du lait coupé*, instead of blood in her veins! And I'll tell you another thing: I confess it's the first time I hear that the man to whom I'm gracious is deserving of pity and playing a miserable part! I know of a more miserable part—that of a man who doesn't know what is going on in his own heart!'

Litvinov drew himself up in his turn.

'Irina,' he began.

But she suddenly pressed both her palms against her forehead, and flinging herself impetuously on his breast embraced him with more than a woman's force.

'Forgive me, forgive me,' she said in a tremulous voice. 'Forgive me, Grigory! You see how spoiled I am, how horrid, jealous, and wicked; you see how I need your help, your indulgence! Yes, save me, pluck me out of this morass before I'm lost in it altogether! Yes, let us escape, escape from these people, from this society, to some distant, free, beautiful land! Perhaps your Irina will at last become more worthy of the sacrifices you are making for her! Don't be angry with me, forgive me, my dear one, and know that I'll do all you tell me, will go wherever you take me!'

Litvinov's heart turned within him. Irina was clinging to him closer than before with her young and supple body. He bent down over her fragrant hair that had come loose and, in the intoxication of gratitude and delight, scarcely dared to caress it with his hand, scarcely touched it with his lips.

'Irina, Irina,' he repeated, 'my angel. . . .'

She suddenly raised her head and listened. 'It's my husband's steps . . . he's gone into his room,' she whispered, and swiftly drawing away moved into an arm-chair. Litvinov rose to go. 'Where are you going?' she continued in the same whisper. 'Stay; he's suspicious of you as it is. Or are you afraid of him?' Her eyes were fixed on the door. 'Yes, it's he; he'll come in here in a minute. Tell me something; talk to me.' Litvinov could not think of anything and remained silent. 'Are you going to the theatre to-morrow?' she said aloud. 'They are doing *Le Verre d'eau*, it's an old-fashioned play and Plessy is frightfully affected. . . . We seem to be in a fever,' she added lowering her voice; 'that won't do; we must think it over properly. I must warn you that all my money is in his hands; *mais j'ai mes bijoux*. Let's go to Spain, shall we?' She raised her voice again. 'I wonder why all actresses grow fat? Take Madeleine Brohan, for instance. . . . But do say something, don't remain silent. My head is going round. But you mustn't doubt me. . . . I'll let you know where you can meet me to-morrow. Only it's a pity you told that young lady. . . . *Ah! mais c'est charmant!*' she exclaimed suddenly, and with a nervous laugh tore the hem off her handkerchief.

'May I come in?' Ratmirov asked from the other room.

'Yes . . . you may.'

The door opened and the general appeared on the threshold. He gave a slight frown on seeing Litvinov, but bowed to him, that is, bent the upper part of his body.

'I didn't know you had a visitor,' he said, '*je vous demande pardon de mon indiscrétion*. Does Baden still amuse you, M'sieur—Litvinov?'

Ratmirov always stumbled over Litvinov's name;

it was as though he forgot it every time, and could not recall it at once.... By doing this, and also by raising his hat too high in greeting, he sought to wound him.

'I'm not bored here, *m'sieur le général.*'

'Indeed? And I'm awfully tired of Baden. We are soon leaving here, aren't we, Irina Pavlovna? *Assez de Bade comme ça.* Though to-day I've won five hundred francs for you.'

Irina coquettishly held out her hand.

'Where are they? May I have them, please? For pin-money.'

'You shall have them, you shall have them.... You're going already, M'sieur—Litvinov?'

'Yes I am, as you see.'

Ratmirov bent his body again.

'Till we meet again!'

'Good-bye, Grigory Mihailitch,' said Irina. 'And I shall keep my promise.'

'What promise? May I be inquisitive?' her husband asked.

Irina smiled.

'No, it's just ... something we've been talking of. *C'est à propos du voyage ... où il vous plaira.* You know—Staël's book?'

'Oh, yes! I know, I know. Charming illustrations.'

Ratmirov seemed to be on the best of terms with his wife.

XXII

'It's better not to think, really,' Litvinov repeated to himself, walking down the street and feeling that the inner turmoil was rising in him again. 'It's settled. She will keep her promise, and it only remains for me to take the necessary steps. . . . But she seems to hesitate. . . .' He tossed his head. His own intentions appeared to him in a strange light: there was something artificial and unreal about them.

One cannot dwell too long upon the same thoughts: they gradually shift, like bits of glass in a kaleidoscope . . . one looks and sees that the images before one's eyes are quite different. A sense of profound weariness descended upon Litvinov . . . he wished he could rest if only for an hour. But Tanya? He roused himself, and without further reasoning submissively walked home; it merely came into his mind that he was all day being tossed like a ball from one to the other. . . . No matter: he had to make an end. He returned to his hotel, and as submissively, almost insensibly, without hesitation or delay, went to Tatyana.

He was met by Kapitolina Markovna. From the first glance at her he understood that she knew everything; the poor maiden lady's eyes were swollen with weeping, and her flushed face, framed by dishevelled white locks, expressed dismay and the anguish of indignation, sorrow, and boundless amazement. She rushed towards Litvinov, but stopped immediately, and, biting her trembling lips looked at him as though she would both implore him and kill him, and assure herself that it was all madness, a dream, an impossible thing, wasn't it?

' So you . . . you 've come, you 've come,' she began. The door into the next room opened instantly, and Tatyana, transparently pale but calm, came with a light step into the room.

She gently embraced her aunt with one arm and made her sit down beside her.

' Sit down too, Grigory Mihailitch,' she said to Litvinov, who stood by the door like one lost. ' I am very glad to be seeing you once more. I have told my aunt your decision, our common decision; she quite agrees with it and approves. . . . Without mutual love there can be no happiness, mutual respect is not enough '—at the word ' respect ' Litvinov involuntarily lowered his eyes —'and it 's better to part now than repent afterwards. Isn't it, aunt? '

' Yes, of course,' Kapitolina Markovna began, ' of course, Tanyusha, a person who cannot appreciate you . . . who ventured to——'

' Aunt, aunt,' Tatyana interrupted her, ' remember what you promised me. You have yourself always said to me, " Truth, truth before all things, Tatyana— and freedom." Well, truth is not always pleasant, nor freedom either; or else, what would our merit be? '

She kissed Kapitolina Markovna tenderly on her white hair, and turning to Litvinov continued:

'We've decided to leave Baden . . . I think that will make it easier for all of us.'

'When do you think of going?' Litvinov brought out in a toneless voice. He recalled that Irina had recently asked him the same question.

Kapitolina Markovna moved forward, but Tatyana restrained her, affectionately touching her shoulder.

'Probably soon, very soon.'

'Will you allow me to ask you where you intend to go?' Litvinov said in the same voice.

'First to Dresden and then probably to Russia.'

'But what do you want to know it for now, Grigory Mihailitch?' Kapitolina Markovna exclaimed.

'Aunt, aunt,' Tatyana interposed again. There was a short silence.

'Tatyana Petrovna,' Litvinov began, 'you understand how bitterly painful and sorrowful my feelings must be at this moment. . . .'

Tatyana got up.

'Don't let us speak of it, Grigory Mihailitch,' she brought out. 'Please don't, I beg you, if not for your sake, then for mine. 'I've known you long enough and can well imagine what you must be feeling now. But what's the good of talking, what's the good of disturbing——' (She paused—she obviously wanted to get over her emotion and hold back the gathering tears; she succeeded.) 'What's the good of disturbing a wound which cannot be healed? Let us leave that to time. And meanwhile I have something to ask of you, Grigory Mihailitch: I'll give you a letter: will you be so kind as to take it to the post yourself, it's rather important, and aunt and I haven't time

197

just now. . . . I'll be very grateful. Wait a minute—
I won't be long.'

In the doorway Tatyana looked round anxiously at
Kapitolina Markovna; but she sat there so sedate
and dignified, with such a stern expression on her
tightly compressed lips and knitted brows that
Tatyana merely nodded to her and went out.

But no sooner was the door closed after her than
all sternness and dignity instantly left Kapitolina
Markovna's face. She got up, ran on tiptoe towards
Litvinov, and bending down and trying to look into
his eyes, spoke in a tremulous, tearful whisper:

'Merciful heavens!' she began, 'Grigory Mihailitch, what's this: a dream, or what? *You* give up
Tanya, you love her no longer, you go back on your
word! You are doing it, Grigory Mihailitch—you,
whom we all trusted implicitly! You? You? You?
You, Grisha?' Kapitolina Markovna paused. 'But
you'll kill her,' she went on, since he made no answer,
and tears ran in small drops down her cheeks. 'She's
putting a bold face on it now, but you mustn't take
any notice of that—you know what she is! She
never complains. She doesn't pity herself, so others
must have pity on her! She keeps telling me, " Aunt,
we must preserve our dignity!"—dignity, indeed,
when I foresee death, yes, death. . . .' (Tatyana
moved her chair in the next room.) 'Yes, I foresee death,' the old lady went on in a still lower
voice. 'And what could have happened? Have you
been bewitched, or what? You've been writing the
tenderest letters to her all the time! And, besides,
an honourable man cannot behave like that! You

know, I am thoroughly unconventional and *esprit fort*, and I've brought Tanya up in that way, she too has a free mind——'

'Aunt!' Tatyana's voice was heard from the next room.

'But a word of honour is binding, Grigory Mihailitch! Especially for people with your, with our, principles! If we don't recognize duty, what will there be left us? One cannot break a promise—simply at one's own whim, without considering how it affects other people! It's dishonourable ... yes, it's a crime—what sort of freedom is that?'

'Aunt, come here, please,' was heard again.

'I'm coming, dear, I'm coming. ...' Kapitolina Markovna seized Litvinov by the hand. 'I see you're angry, Grigory Mihailitch. ...' ('I? I angry?' he wanted to call out, but his tongue would not obey him.) 'I don't want to make you angry. Goodness me, I have no thoughts to spare for that! On the contrary, I want to implore you: come to your senses while there's still time—don't ruin her, don't ruin your own happiness, she will still believe you. Grisha, she'll believe you, nothing is lost yet; why, she loves you as no one will ever love you! Leave this hateful Baden-Baden, let's go away together, only escape from this enchantment, and the chief thing, have pity, have pity——'

'Aunt!' Tatyana called with a shade of impatience in her voice.

But Kapitolina Markovna was not heeding her.

'Only say yes,' she kept repeating to Litvinov, 'and I'll arrange it all. ... Well, at least nod your head! Just nod your head, dear, like this, just once!'

Litvinov would readily have died at that moment; but he did not say yes or nod his head.

Tatyana came in with the letter in her hand. Kapitolina Markovna instantly jumped away from Litvinov and, averting her face, bent low over the table, as though examining the bills and papers that lay on it.

Tatyana walked up to Litvinov.

'Here,' she said, 'is the letter I spoke of. . . . You'll go to the post at once, won't you?'

Litvinov raised his eyes. . . . Indeed, it was his judge standing before him. Tatyana seemed to him taller and more slender; her face, lit up with a new, strange beauty, had the majestic immobility of a statue; her bosom did not heave, and her dress, of one colour and straight as a tunic, fell in long plain folds of marble drapery to her feet which it covered. Tatyana looked straight before her, at Litvinov alone, and her gaze, cold and impassive, was also the gaze of a statue. He read his sentence in it; he bowed, took the letter from the hand that held it out to him without moving, and withdrew in silence.

Kapitolina Markovna rushed to Tatyana, who drew away from her embrace and lowered her eyes; a flush spread over her face and she went back to the bedroom, saying, 'And now we must make haste!' Kapitolina Markovna followed, hanging her head.

The letter given by Tatyana to Litvinov was addressed to a Dresden friend of hers, a German lady, who let small furnished apartments. Litvinov put it into the letter-box, and it seemed to him that together with this scrap of paper he put all his past, all his life, into the grave. He went out of the town and spent a long time wandering about the narrow paths between vineyards. He could not get rid of a feeling of self-contempt, persistent as the buzzing of a tiresome summer fly: the part he had played at that last meeting was unenviable indeed. . . . When he returned to his hotel and, after a time, inquired after the ladies, he was told that as soon as he had left they had given orders to be driven to the railway station and set off by the mail train to an unknown destination. Their things had been packed and their bills paid since the morning. Tatyana had evidently asked Litvinov to take her letter to the post in order to get him out of the way. He tried to inquire of the porter whether the ladies had left a note for him, but the porter said no, and, indeed, expressed surprise; it was clear that this sudden departure from lodgings engaged a week in advance struck him too as strange and suspicious. Litvinov turned his back on him and shut himself in his room.

He did not leave it till the following day. Most of the night he spent at the table, writing and tearing up what he had written. . . . The dawn was breaking when he finished his work—it was a letter to Irina.

XXIII

THIS is what his letter to Irina said:

My betrothed went away yesterday; she and I will never see each other. . . . I don't even know for certain where she is going to live. She carried away with her all that had hitherto seemed to me precious and desirable; all my plans, decisions, intentions have disappeared with her; my labours are lost, my work of years has turned to nothing, my pursuits have no meaning and no application; all that is dead; my self, my former self is dead and buried since yesterday. I feel that clearly, I see it, I know it—and I don't regret it in the least. It isn't in order to complain that I'm saying this to you. . . . How could I complain when you love me, Irina! I only wanted to tell you that out of all that dead past, out of all those hopes and beginnings, now turned to smoke and dust, one thing only has remained living and unconquerable: my love for you. I have nothing left me except this love, it is all I have; to call it my only treasure wouldn't be sufficient: the whole of me is in that love, that love is my whole being; in it is my future, my vocation, my country, and all that I hold sacred! You know me, Irina, you know that I am not one to use fine phrases —I hate them; however strong the words in which I try to express my feeling may be, you will not doubt their sincerity or think them exaggerated. I'm not a boy impulsively pouring out thoughtless vows in a moment of passing ecstasy, but a man tried in years, telling you simply and directly, almost with terror, what he has recognized for unmistakable truth. Yes, your love has taken the place of all else for me—all, all! Judge for yourself, then: can I leave that *all* in the hands of another? Can I allow him to dispose of you? You—you will belong to him, my very being, my heart's blood will belong to him—and I myself— where shall I be? What shall I be? Thrust aside, an onlooker . . . looking at my own life! No, that's impossible—impossible! To have a part, a secret part in that without which one cannot live, has nothing to live for—that's falsity and death. I know what a tremendous sacrifice I demand of you, without any right to do so; and indeed what can give one a right to sacrifice? It isn't out of selfishness I am doing it: an egoist would find it easier and more comfortable not to raise this question at all. Yes, my demands are heavy and I shall not be surprised if they frighten you. The people among whom you have to live are hateful to you, you are tired of society, but are you strong enough to give up that society, to trample upon the crown it has bestowed upon you, to set public opinion against you, the opinion of those hateful people? Question yourself, Irina, don't take up a burden beyond your strength. I don't want to reproach you, but remember: you succumbed to the temptation once already. There is so little I can give you in exchange for what you'll lose! Now listen to my final word: if you don't feel capable of leaving everything at once, the very next day, and following me—you see how boldly I speak, how little I spare myself—if you are afraid of an uncertain future, of the solitude and estrangement and public censure, in short, if you are uncertain of yourself—tell me candidly and at once and I will go away; I'll go away with a bleeding heart, but I shall bless you for your truthfulness. But if you, my beautiful, radiant queen, do really love an obscure and humble man like me and are really ready to share my lot—well, then give me your hand and let us set out together on our arduous journey. But you must know: my decision is irrevocable: all or nothing! It's madness . . . but I can no other, I can't, Irina! I love you too much. Your G. L.

Litvinov did not very much like this letter; it did not express his meaning quite correctly and adequately; awkward phrases occurred in it, bookish or high flown, and it certainly was not better than many other letters which he had torn up; but it happened to be the last one he wrote, the main thing was stated in it after all—and Litvinov, weary and exhausted, did not feel equal to producing anything else. Besides, he had not the skill of expressing his thoughts in a literary form and, like all people unused to writing, he took trouble over the style. The first letter he wrote was probably the best: it came more directly from the heart. But anyway Litvinov sent his missive to Irina.

She answered him with a short note:

Come to me to-day [she wrote], *he* has gone out for the day. I am very much disturbed by your letter. I think and think . . . and my head is in a turmoil with thinking. I am horribly depressed, but you love me, and I am happy. Come. Your Irina.

She was sitting in her boudoir when Litvinov came in. He was brought in by that same girl of thirteen who had watched for him on the stairs the day before. A semicircular cardboard box of lace stood open on the table before Irina; she was carelessly turning the lace over with one hand, while in the other she held

Litvinov's letter. She had been crying: her eyelashes were wet and her eyelids swollen; her cheeks showed traces of unwiped tears. Litvinov stopped in the doorway: she had not noticed his coming.

'You're crying?' he said in surprise.

She started, passed her hand over her hair, and smiled.

'Why are you crying?' Litvinov repeated. She silently pointed to the letter. 'So that's the reason,' he brought out slowly.

'Come here, sit down,' she said. 'Give me your hand. Well, yes, I've been crying. Why should it surprise you? Do you suppose *this* is easy?' She pointed to the letter again.

Litvinov sat down.

'I know it isn't easy, Irina, that's just what I say in my letter . . . I understand your position. But if you recognize what your love means to me, if my words have convinced you, you must also understand what I feel at the sight of your tears. I've come here to hear my verdict and am waiting: what is it to be? Death or life? Your answer will decide everything. Only don't look at me with such eyes. . . . They remind me of your eyes in those days in Moscow.'

Irina blushed suddenly and turned away as though herself feeling that something was amiss in her gaze.

'What are you saying, Grigory? For shame! You want to know my answer . . . as though you could doubt it! You are disturbed by my tears, but you've misunderstood them. Your letter, dearest, has made me wonder. . . . Here you write that my love has re-placed everything for you, that even your former studies will now be useless; and I am asking myself, can man live by love alone? Won't he be tired of it at last, won't he long for activity and blame that which drew him away from it? That 's the thought that frightens me, that 's what I fear, and not what you suppose.'

Litvinov looked intently at Irina, and she looked intently at him, as though each wished to penetrate deeper and further into the other's mind, deeper and further than words can either express or reach.

' You needn't be afraid of that,' Litvinov began. ' I must have expressed myself badly. Boredom? Inactivity? With the fresh powers that your love will give me? Oh, Irina, believe me, your love is a whole world to me, and I can't yet myself foresee what may develop from it ! '

Irina pondered.

' Where shall we go? ' she whispered.

' Where? We 'll talk of that presently. But then—then you agree, you agree, Irina? '

She looked at him. ' And you 'll be happy? '

' Oh, Irina ! '

' You won't regret anything? Never? '

She bent down to the box and again began turning over the lace in it.

' Don't be annoyed with me, darling, for busying myself with this rubbish at such a moment. . . . I have to go to a ball at a certain lady's, these rags have been sent me and I must choose to-day. Oh, I am horribly wretched ! ' she cried out suddenly and leaned her face against the edge of the box. Tears began to fall from her eyes again. She turned away: the tears might drop on the lace.

'Irina, you're crying again——' Litvinov began uneasily.

'Well, yes, again,' Irina interposed. 'Oh, Grigory, don't torment me, don't torment yourself! Let us be free people! What does it matter that I'm crying? I don't know myself why my tears are flowing. You know my decision, you've heard it, you're certain it won't change, that I agree to—how did you put it?—to all or nothing. . . . What more do you want? Let us be free! Why put each other in fetters? We are alone now, you love me, I love you—surely we've something better to do than ferret out each other's thoughts? Look at me: I didn't want to pose before you, I didn't hint by a single word that perhaps it wasn't so easy for me to trample on my duties as a wife. . . and I don't deceive myself, I know I am a criminal, and *he* has a right to kill me. Well, what of it! Let's be free, I say. A day is a lifetime.'

She got up from her chair and looked down on Litvinov, smiling faintly, screwing up her eyes and with her arm bare to the elbow pushing away from her face a long lock of hair on which two or three tears glistened. A gorgeous lace fichu slipped off the table and fell on the floor at her feet. She trampled on it contemptuously. 'Don't I please you to-day? Have I grown plain since yesterday? Tell me, have you often seen a more beautiful arm? And this hair? Tell me, do you love me?'

She threw both arms round him, pressed his head to her bosom, her comb fell out with a ringing sound, and her loosened hair covered him like a soft and fragrant wave.

XXIV

LITVINOV paced up and down his room at the hotel, his head bowed in thought. He had now to pass from theory to practice, to find ways and means for their elopement, for moving to unknown lands. . . . But strange to say, instead of thinking of those ways and means he kept asking himself whether the decision upon which he so firmly insisted had been really, indubitably taken. Had the final, irrevocable word been said? Irina certainly did say to him as they parted: ' Make all the arrangements, and when you are ready, merely let me know.' It was settled! There was no room for doubt. . . . He had to begin on his task. And he began, meanwhile, by considering matters. In the first place, money. Litvinov found that he had in hand 1328 guldens, in French currency 2855 francs; it was not much, but enough for their first needs; then he must write to his father and ask him to send as much as possible, to sell the forest and part of the land. . . . But under what pretext? Oh, a pretext could be found right enough. Irina had spoken, it's true, of her *bijoux*; but that should on no account be taken into consideration; who knows, that might come in useful for a rainy day. Then he had by him a good Geneva watch which might fetch . . . say, 400 francs.

Litvinov went to a banker and cautiously approached

208

the question whether it was possible in case of need to obtain a loan; but bankers in Baden are wary and sorely tried men, and on hearing such indirect inquiries immediately assume a faded and drooping appearance, exactly like a field flower mown down by the scythe; others, on the contrary, boldly and cheerfully laugh in your face as though appreciating your innocent joke. . . .

Litvinov, to his shame, actually tried his luck at roulette, actually put a thaler — shocking to relate!—on number 30, corresponding to his age. He did this in order to increase and round off his capital; and though he did not increase it, he certainly rounded it off by losing the odd twenty-eight guldens.

The second question, also an important one, was that of the passport. But for a woman it was not strictly obligatory, and there were countries where it was not required at all: Belgium, for instance, and England; besides, one might obtain a passport that was not Russian. Litvinov reflected about all this very seriously; his determination was firm, without a trace of wavering; and yet, apart from his will, against his will, something frivolous, almost comical, crept into his reflections as though his plan were a joke, as though no one ever eloped with any one in reality, but only in farces and novels, or perhaps in the depths of the country, in the wilds of provincial Russia where, according to one traveller's testimony, people are sometimes sick through sheer boredom. It came into Litvinov's mind how a friend of his, a retired cornet, Batsov, carried away in a hired chaise, with bells and a troika,[1] a merchant's daughter, having first made the parents drunk, and the girl too—and how it appeared afterwards that it was he who had been duped and very nearly got a thrashing into the bargain. Litvinov was extremely annoyed with himself for such unsuitable recollections, and remembering Tatyana, her sudden departure and all that sorrow, suffering, and shame, poignantly felt that what he had undertaken was no joking matter, and that he was perfectly right when he told Irina that his very honour left him no other way out. . . . And again at her mere name something fiery instantly twined itself round his heart and died down with blissful pain.

He heard horses' hoofs behind him . . . he stepped aside. Irina on horseback overtook him; the stout general was riding beside her. She recognized Litvinov, nodded to him, and striking her horse with the whip put it into a gallop and suddenly set off at full speed. Her dark veil fluttered in the wind.

' *Pas si vite! Nom de Dieu! Pas si vite!* ' the general shouted as he galloped after her.

---

[1] A team of three horses abreast.   (Translator's note.)

XXV

The following morning, just as Litvinov returned to his hotel from the banker with whom he had had another talk about the playful variability of our exchange and the best means of sending money abroad, the hall-porter handed him a letter. He recognized Irina's handwriting and without breaking the seal—a foreboding of evil, heaven only knows why, stirred within him—went to his room. This was what he read (the letter was written in French):

Dearest! I 've been thinking of your plan all through the night. . . . I will not try to deceive you. You 've been frank with me, and I 'll be frank too; I *cannot* run away with you, *I haven't the strength* to do it. I feel how deeply I am wronging you—my second guilt is even greater than the first—I despise myself, my cowardice, I reproach myself bitterly, but I cannot change my nature. In vain do I say to myself that I 've ruined your happiness, that you really have a right now to regard me as merely a frivolous coquette, that I proposed it myself and gave you solemn promises. . . . I 'm horrified, I hate myself, but I can't help it, I can't, I can't. I don't want to justify myself, I 'm not going to say that I too have been carried away . . . all that doesn't mean anything; but I want to tell you and repeat again and again: I 'm yours, yours for ever, dispose of me as you will, when you will, without any conditions, any obligations, I am yours. . . . But to

run away, to throw up everything! . . . no! no! no!
I implored you to save me, I hoped to blot out
everything, to burn up everything as with fire . . . but
I see there is no salvation for me; I see the poison has
penetrated into me too deeply; I see one cannot with
impunity breathe that air for years and years! I 've
long hesitated about writing this letter to you, I 'm
frightened to think what your decision may be, I rely
only on your love for me. But I thought it would
be dishonourable of me not to tell you the truth—
especially as you may perhaps have begun to take steps
to carry out our plan. Ah! it was beautiful—but
impossible. Oh, my darling, think of me as a weak,
frivolous woman, despise me, but don't forsake me,
don't forsake your Irina! . . . I haven't the strength
to give up this society, but I cannot live in it without
you. We shall soon be returning to Petersburg, come
there, live there, we 'll find work for you, your former
labours shall not be wasted, you 'll find a useful
application for them . . . only live near me, only love
me, such as I am, with all my weaknesses and vices,
and know that no heart will ever be devoted to you
as tenderly as the heart of your Irina. Come to me
as soon as you can, I shan't have a minute's peace
until I see you.

Your, your, your, Irina.

Like a sledge-hammer Litvinov's blood beat in
his head and then slowly and heavily sank on to his
heart and remained there, a dead weight of stone.
He read Irina's letter once more and, as that time in
Moscow, threw himself on the sofa in utter exhaustion
and remained motionless. A dark abyss seemed suddenly to have opened on all sides of him, and he
gazed into that darkness unmeaningly and in despair.

And so it was deceit again—no, worse than deceit—falsehood and baseness. . . . His life was wrecked, all was torn up by the roots, utterly, and the only thing to which he still could cling—his last support—that too was broken into fragments!

'Come after us to Petersburg,' he repeated to himself with bitter inner laughter. 'We'll find work for you there.'. . . 'Will they appoint me a head clerk, or what? And who are those "we"? This is where her past has come to the surface—that secret, hideous past which I don't know and which she has tried to blot out, to burn as in a fire! This is that world of intrigues, secret connections, dark stories of Belskys and Dolskys. . . . And what a future, what a lovely part in store for me! To live close to her, visit her, share with her the corrupt melancholy of a fashionable lady who finds society a burden and a bore, but cannot exist without it; to be a family friend to her and, of course, to his excellency . . . until . . . until the caprice is over and the plebeian friend loses his piquancy and is replaced by the stout general or by Mr. Finikov—that's possible, and pleasant, and perhaps even useful . . . she talks of the "useful application" of my abilities!—while the other plan is impossible! Impossible!'

Like sudden gusts of wind before a storm impulses of wild fury rose up in Litvinov's heart. . . . Every phrase in Irina's letter roused his indignation, her very protestations of her love being unchangeable offended him. 'I can't leave it like that,' he cried out at last. 'I won't allow her to play with my life so pitilessly. . . .'

He jumped up and seized his hat. But what was he

to do? Run to her? Answer her letter? He stood still and his hands fell.

Yes: what was he to do?

Had he not himself offered her the fatal choice? It had not turned out as he wished ... but every choice is subject to that danger. True, she had changed her mind; she had been the first to tell him that she would throw up everything and follow him— that was true also; but then she did not deny that she was to blame, she plainly said that she was a weak woman; she did not want to deceive him, she was deceived in herself. . . . What answer was there to that? At any rate she did not shuffle, she did not pretend . . . she was frank with him, mercilessly frank. There was no need for her to speak out at once, there was nothing to prevent her lulling him with promises, putting things off and leaving him in ignorance till her very departure . . . departure with her husband to Italy ! But she had ruined his life, she had ruined two lives ! . . . Well, such things happened.

And it was not she who had wronged Tatyana, but he, Litvinov, and he had no right to shake off the responsibility which his guilt had laid upon him like an iron yoke. . . . All that was true; but what was he to do now?

He threw himself on the sofa again, and again moments rushed by with devouring swiftness, dark and meaningless, leaving no trace.

' Or shall I do what she says? ' flashed through his mind. ' She loves me, she is mine, and isn't there something inevitable, irresistible like a law of nature in our very attraction to each other, in this passion which after so many years has broken out and asserted itself with such force? Live in Petersburg ... I wouldn't be the first to be in that position. And, besides, where could she and I have found a home? '

He sank into thought, and the image of Irina, as it had for ever imprinted itself in his memory during those last few days, gently appeared before him. . . .

But it was not for long. He recovered himself and with a new burst of indignation drove away from his mind both the memory and the seductive image.

' You give me to drink out of that golden cup,' he cried out, ' but there's poison in your draught, and your white wings are soiled with mire. . . . Begone ! To remain here with you, after I had . . . driven away my betrothed . . . that's dishonourable ! Dishonourable !'

He clenched his hands in misery, and another face, with the stamp of suffering on its set features and silent reproach in the farewell glance, rose out of the depths.

For a long time Litvinov endured this agony; for a long time his tortured thought, like a sick man in a fever, tossed from side to side. He calmed down at last; at last he made up his mind. He had felt from the very first moment what his decision would be ... it had appeared before him, to begin with, like a distant point, scarcely perceptible in the dark whirlwind of his inward struggle; then it had moved nearer and nearer and ended by cutting like a cold blade into his heart.

Litvinov again pulled his trunk out of the corner, again packed all his things, without hurry and even indeed with a kind of dull carefulness, rang for the waiter, paid his bill, and sent Irina the following note in Russian:

'I don't know whether you have wronged me more this time than the last; but I know that this present blow is much heavier. It is the end. You tell me "I cannot," and I repeat the same thing to you: I cannot ... do what you wish. I cannot and I don't want to. Don't answer me. You are unable to give me the only answer I would accept. Good-bye, and may you be happy.... We shall probably not see each other again.'

Litvinov did not leave his room all the evening; whether he was waiting for anything heaven only knows. About seven o'clock in the evening a lady in a black cloak with a veil over her face came up twice to the steps of his hotel. She walked away a few paces and, after gazing into the distance, suddenly made a resolute movement with her hand, and for the third time went towards the steps.

'Where are you going, Irina Pavlovna?' a strained voice said behind her.

She turned swiftly round.... Potugin was running to her.

She stopped, thought a moment, and then rushing towards him, took his arm and drew him away.

'Take me away, take me away,' she repeated breathlessly.

'What's the matter with you, Irina Pavlovna?' he muttered in amazement.

'Take me away,' she repeated with redoubled force, 'if you don't want me to remain for ever ... there!'

Potugin obediently bowed his head and they hastily walked away together.

Early the following morning—when Litvinov was just setting off on his journey—Potugin came into his room.

He approached Litvinov in silence and shook hands with him. Litvinov did not say anything either. Both had long faces and both vainly tried to smile.

' I 've come to wish you a pleasant journey,' Potugin brought out at last.

' And how do you know that I 'm going away to-day? ' Litvinov asked.

Potugin looked on the floor about him. ' It 's come to my knowledge . . . as you see. Our last conversation took such a strange turn. . . . I shouldn't like to part from you without expressing my sincere regard for you.'

' You feel it now . . . when I'm going away? '

Potugin looked sadly at Litvinov. ' Ah, Grigory Mihailitch,' he began with a short sigh, ' we have no thoughts to spare now for these subtleties and arguments. So far as I 've noticed you don't much care for ancient Russian literature and perhaps haven't heard about Vaska Buslaev? '

' About whom? '

' Vaska Buslaev, a hero of Novgorod—in Kirsha Danilov's anthology.'

' What Buslaev? ' Litvinov brought out, somewhat taken aback by this unexpected turn in the conversation. ' I don't know.'

' Well, never mind. This is what I wanted you to

observe. This Vaska Buslaev enticed his Novgorod men on a pilgrimage to Jerusalem and, to their horror, bathed naked in the holy river of Jordan, for he " believed not in dreams nor signs nor the call of birds." This logical Vaska Buslaev climbed Mount Tabor, at the top of which lay a big stone, which all kinds of men had vainly tried to jump over. . . . Vaska too wanted to try his luck. On his way he came across a death's-head, a human skull, and kicked it away. So the death's-head said to him: " Why do you kick me? I knew how to live and I know how to lie in the dust—and the same thing will happen to you." And, indeed, Vaska tried to jump over the stone and when he had nearly succeeded he caught his heel in it and broke his head. And at this point I must remark that it wouldn't be amiss for my friends the Slavophils, who are very fond of kicking death's-heads and decaying nations, to ponder over this legend.'

' But what's your point? ' Litvinov interrupted him impatiently at last. ' It's time I was going, you must excuse me——'

' My point is,' Potugin answered, and his eyes lit up with a feeling so friendly that Litvinov had not expected it of him, ' my point is that you, now, do not kick away a dead human head, and perhaps for your goodness you 'll succeed in jumping over the fatal stone. I won't detain you any more, only allow me to embrace you before you go.'

' I won't even attempt to jump,' Litvinov said, exchanging with Potugin the traditional three kisses, and to the sorrowful feelings overflowing his heart there was added for a moment pity for the lonely,

unhappy man. 'But I must be going, I must. . . . '
He bustled about the room.

' Shall I carry something for you? ' Potugin offered.

' No, thank you, don't trouble, I'll manage. . . .'
He put on his cap, took his bag in his hands. ' And
so,' he asked standing in the doorway, ' you say
you've seen her? '

' Yes, I have.'

' Well . . . and how is she? '

Potugin paused. ' She expected you yesterday . . .
and will expect you to-day.'

' Ah! Tell her then—— No, there's no need, no
need to say anything. Good-bye. . . . Good-bye! '

' Good-bye, Grigory Mihailitch. . . . Let me say one
more thing to you. You have time to listen to me:
there's more than half an hour before your train goes.
You are returning to Russia . . . you will . . . work
there . . . in time. Allow then an old babbler—for,
alas, I am nothing but a babbler—to give you a piece
of advice on parting. Each time you begin on something new, ask yourself whether you are serving
civilization—in the true and strict sense of the word—
whether you are realizing one of its principles, whether
your activity is of that European, educative kind which
alone is useful and fruitful in our time among us. If
yes, go boldly forward: you are on the right path and
your work is blessed! Thank God, you are not alone
now. You will not be a " solitary sower "; there are
now real workers . . . pioneers, among us too. But
you have no time for this now. Good-bye, don't
forget me! '

Litvinov ran down the stairs, jumped into the

carriage, and drove to the station without once looking back at the town where so much of his own life was left. . . . It was as though he had given himself up to a wave: it caught him up and bore him along, and he was firmly determined not to resist it . . . he had given up all other attempts to assert his will.

He was getting into the carriage.

'Grigory Mihailovitch . . . Grigory . . .' he heard an imploring whisper behind him.

He shuddered. . . . Could it be Irina? Yes, it was she. Wrapped up in her maid's shawl, a travelling hat on her disarranged hair, she stood on the platform looking at him with lustreless eyes. 'Come back, come back, I've come for you,' those eyes said. And what, what promises they held out! She did not move, she had not the strength to say another word; everything in her, the very disorder of her dress, seemed to be begging for mercy.

Litvinov staggered and very nearly rushed to her. . . . But the wave to which he had surrendered himself held its own. . . . He jumped into the carriage, and turning round, motioned Irina to the seat next to him. She understood him. There was still time. Only one step, one movement, and two lives united for ever would have sped away into the unknown distance. . . . While she hesitated a loud whistle blew and the train started.

Litvinov sank back, and Irina walked unsteadily to a seat and fell on it, to the amazement of a retired diplomatist who had accidentally strayed into the station. He knew Irina very little but was much interested in her, and seeing that she lay there as though in a faint thought that she had *une attaque de nerfs* and considered it his duty as *un galant chevalier* to come to her aid. He was still more amazed, however, when at the first word he addressed to her she got up suddenly, pushed away his proffered arm, and running out into the street instantly disappeared in the milky white mist, characteristic of the Black Forest climate in the early days of autumn.

XXVI

It happened to us once to come into the cottage of a
peasant woman who had just lost her only, dearly
beloved son, and to our considerable surprise to find
her quite calm and almost gay. 'Don't disturb her,'
said her husband who probably noticed our surprise,
'she's gone numb now.'—Litvinov, too, had 'gone
numb.' The same kind of deadly calm descended
upon him during the first hours of his journey.
Utterly crushed and hopelessly miserable as he was, he
was resting, resting after the torments and anxieties
of the previous week, after all the blows that had
fallen one after another upon his head. He was all
the more shaken by them because he was not made for
such storms. Now he really hoped for nothing, and
tried not to think of the past—above all, not to think
of the past. He was going to Russia . . . he had to do
something with himself! but he no longer made any
plans concerning his own personal life. He did not
recognize himself; he did not understand his actions;
it was as though he had lost his real self, and indeed
he took little interest in that self. Sometimes it
seemed to him that he was taking his own corpse
home, and only the occasional bitter spasms or irreme-
diable mental anguish reminded him that he was still
burdened with life. At times it seemed to him impossible that a man—a man !—could allow himself to

be so influenced by a woman, by love. . . . 'Contemptible weakness,' he whispered, and he shook his overcoat and settled down more firmly in his seat as though to say: 'The past is over now, let's begin afresh. . . .' A moment later he merely smiled bitterly and wondered at himself.

He began looking out of the carriage window. The day was damp and grey, there was no rain, but the mist persisted and low clouds covered the sky. There was a head wind; whitish billows of steam, separately or mixed with the darker clouds of smoke, rushed in an endless procession past the window by which Litvinov sat. He began watching this steam and smoke. Continually mounting, rising and falling, twirling round, and catching at the grass and the bushes, as though in grotesque play, the billows followed one another, stretching out and melting away . . . they changed perpetually and remained the same . . . a hurried, dull, monotonous game ! Sometimes the railway track curved, the wind changed—the whole mass vanished suddenly and at once reappeared at the opposite window; then again the huge tail switched over and again blotted out Litvinov's view of the broad plain by the Rhine. He gazed and gazed, and suddenly a strange reflection came into his mind. . . . He was alone in the compartment; there was no one to disturb him. ' Smoke, smoke,' he repeated several times: and it suddenly seemed to him that everything was smoke: everything—his own life, Russian life, everything human, especially everything Russian. ' All is vapour and smoke,' he thought; ' all seems to change continually, everywhere new forms appear, events follow upon events, but at bottom all is the same; everything hurries, hastens somewhere —and everything disappears without a trace, attaining nothing; the wind changes—and everything rushes in the opposite direction, and there the same unceasing, restless, and futile game begins again.' He recalled much that happened with clamour and commotion before his eyes of late years. . . . ' Smoke,' he whispered, 'smoke.' He recalled the heated arguments, shouts, and discussions at Gubaryov's and at other people's, young and old, humble and highly placed, advanced and reactionary. . . . ' Smoke,' he repeated, ' vapour and smoke.' He recalled at last the memorable picnic, recalled other speeches and pronouncements of other would-be statesmen—and even all that Potugin had preached . . . smoke, smoke, and nothing more. And what of his own strivings and feelings and endeavours and dreams? He merely made a gesture of despair.

And meanwhile the train ran on and on; Rastadt and Carlsruhe and Bruchsal had long been left behind; the mountains on the right of the line receded into the distance, then drew nearer again, but they were not so high and less wooded. The train turned sharply aside . . . here was Heidelberg. The carriages rolled into the roofed station; there were shouts of newsvendors, selling all sorts of magazines including Russian ones; the travellers bustled in their seats and came out on to the platform. But Litvinov did not leave his corner and sat on, hanging his head. Suddenly someone called him by name; he raised his eyes; Bindasov's ugly face thrust itself in at the window, and behind him—or was it his fancy?—no, really, they were all familiar, Baden faces: Madame Suhanchikov, Voroshilov, Bambaev; they were all moving up to him, and Bindasov was shouting:

'And where's Pishchalkin? We were expecting him; but never mind, come along, you sniveller, we're all going to Gubaryov's.'

'Yes, yes, brother, Gubaryov is expecting us,' Bambaev confirmed, stepping forward. 'Come along.'

Litvinov would have been angry but for the dead weight on his heart. He glanced at Bindasov and turned away in silence.

'Do you hear, Gubaryov is here!' Madame Suhanchikov shrieked and her eyes nearly jumped out of her head.

Litvinov did not stir.

'But look here, Litvinov,' Bambaev began, 'there's not only Gubaryov here, there's a whole crowd of the finest, most intelligent Russian young men—and they are all studying natural sciences, and all have such noble convictions! Why, you ought to come if only for their sake! There's, for instance, a certain —there, I've forgotten his name—but he is simply a genius!'

'Leave him alone, leave him alone,' Madame Suhanchikov intervened. 'Don't bother about him! You see what sort of man he is; and his whole family is like that. He has an aunt: I thought at first she was a sensible woman, but the other day I was travelling with her here—she had only just come to Baden, and, behold, was already rushing back—well, we were in the train together and I began asking her questions. . . .

Would you believe it, I couldn't get a word out of the stuck-up creature. Horrid aristocrat!'

Poor Kapitolina Markovna—an aristocrat! Could she have expected such a humiliation?

But Litvinov remained silent; he pulled his cap over his eyes and turned away. The train moved at last.

'Say something by way of good-bye, you stony man!' Bambaev called out, 'that's not the way to behave!'

'Milksop! Ninny!' Bindasov roared. The carriages were moving faster and faster, and he could swear with impunity. 'Skinflint! Slug! Muckworm!'

Whether Bindasov invented this last term of abuse on the spot, or had learnt it from others, it greatly pleased two of the noblest young men studying natural sciences who happened to be present, and a few days later it appeared in a Russian periodical published at that time at Heidelberg under the title *A tout venant je crache!* or 'We'll turn up trumps.'[1]

And Litvinov again began repeating the same old word: 'Smoke, smoke, smoke! Here,' he thought, 'there are over a hundred Russian students at Heidelberg; they are all learning physics, chemistry, physiology, and won't hear of anything else ... but in another five or six years not fifteen will listen to the same renowned professors ... the wind will change, the smoke will blow in another direction ... smoke ... smoke ... smoke!'[2]

---

[1] A historical fact.

[2] Litvinov's presentiment was justified: in 1866 the number of Russian students at Heidelberg was thirteen in the summer, and twelve in the winter term.

Towards nightfall he passed by Cassel. Together with the darkness unendurable anguish swooped down upon him like a hawk, and he wept, huddled away in his corner. His tears flowed long, not lightening his heart, but tormenting it with a kind of bitter, corroding pain; and meanwhile at one of the Cassel hotels Tatyana lay in bed, sick with fever; Kapitolina Markovna sat beside her.

'Tanya,' she said, 'for God's sake let me send a telegram to Grigory Mihailovitch; let me, Tanya!'

'No, aunt,' she answered, 'there's no need to, don't be alarmed. Give me some water; I shall soon be better.'

And indeed a week later she recovered, and the two friends continued their journey.

XXVII

WITHOUT stopping in Petersburg or Moscow Litvinov returned to his estate. He was alarmed to see how much feebler in mind and body his father had grown. The old man was glad to see his son, so far as one who has done with life can feel gladness; he at once handed over to him the management of the estate which was in great disorder, and after lingering for a few more weeks departed this life. Litvinov was left alone in the master's tumbledown lodge, and, with a heavy heart, without hope, without enthusiasm, and without money, began farming. Farming in Russia is not a cheerful affair, as many of us know only too well; there is no need to describe how hard Litvinov found it. There could, of course, be no question of reforms and innovations; the practical application of knowledge acquired abroad had to be put off for an indefinite time; lack of money made it imperative to struggle on from day to day, and to accept all kinds of compromises—both material and moral. The new principles had not taken root, the old had lost all force; inexperience clashed with unscrupulousness; the whole structure of life, shaken to its foundations, shook and quivered like a bog, and only the great word 'freedom' moved like the spirit of God upon the waters. Patience was required in the first instance—not passive but active, insistent patience, coupled with skill and sometimes with cunning. . . . Litvinov's state of mind made things doubly difficult for him. There was little of the will to live left in him . . . how was he to have the will to bustle about and work?

But a year passed, then another, and a third one began. The great idea was gradually being realized, clothing itself with flesh and blood; young shoots came from the scattered seed, and enemies—open or secret—could no longer stamp them out. Though Litvinov ended by letting most of his land to the peasants in exchange for labour, that is, by reverting to a poor, primitive system of farming, he succeeded in a few of his plans: he reopened the factory, started a tiny farm with five hired labourers—and he had tried forty in succession—paid off the chief private debts. . . . And he grew stronger in spirit, too; he was more like his former self. True, a deeply hidden feeling of sadness never left him; he was too quiet for his years, he shut himself up within his narrow circle and cut off all his former ties . . . but the deadly indifference had gone and he again acted and moved among living people as one of them. Gone also were the last traces of the enchantment that had possessed him: all that had happened in Baden seemed to him like a dream. . . . And Irina? She too had faded out and disappeared, and Litvinov merely had a vague sense of something dangerous under the mist which gradually enveloped her image. News of Tatyana reached him occasionally; he knew that she had settled with her aunt on her small estate, some two hundred miles away, that she lived very quietly, went out little, and received scarcely any visitors—but was serene and well.

One lovely day in May he was sitting in his study glancing indifferently through the last number of a Petersburg magazine; his servant came in and announced the arrival of his old uncle. That uncle was Kapitolina Markovna's first cousin and had recently been to see her. He had bought an estate near Litvinov's and was on his way to it. He spent a day and a night at his nephew's and told him much about Tatyana's manner of life. The day after he left, Litvinov sent a letter to her, the first after their parting. He asked permission to resume their friendship if only by correspondence, and also wished to know whether he must give up for ever the idea of seeing her some time. He waited for her answer with some agitation . . . the answer came at last. Tatyana responded cordially to his query. ' If you feel like coming to see us some day,' she said at the end of her letter, ' you will be very welcome: it is said that even the sick are better together than apart.' Kapitolina Markovna sent her greetings.

Litvinov was as glad as a child; it was long since anything had made his heart beat so joyfully. He suddenly felt bright and at ease, just as when the sun rises and dispels, the darkness of night, a light breeze runs together with the sunbeams over the face of the awakened earth. Litvinov kept smiling all that day, even when he walked round his farm and gave orders. He immediately began preparing for the journey, and a fortnight later was on his way to Tatyana.

XXVIII

He travelled slowly, by the side-roads, without any special adventures; once a tyre broke on his back wheel; the blacksmith spent no end of time trying to mend it, but finally gave it up, swearing both at the tyre and at himself; fortunately, it appeared, one could travel beautifully along our roads with a broken tyre, especially ' on soft ground,' that is, through mud. Litvinov had two or three rather curious encounters on his journey. At one of the stations a sessional meeting of the ' arbitrators of the peace ' was in progress, and among them was Pishchalkin, who produced on him the impression of a Solomon or a Solon: his utterances were full of such lofty wisdom, and the respect with which both the landowners and the peasants regarded him was so boundless. . . . In appearance, too, Pishchalkin resembled an ancient sage; the top of his head was now quite bald, and his face had grown fatter and set in a kind of pompous jelly of utterly unrestrained virtue. He congratulated Litvinov on arriving '. . . in my own district, if I may venture to use so ambitious a phrase,' and thereupon subsided into silence, overcome by an access of well-intentioned feelings. He did succeed, however, in telling Litvinov one piece of news—and that was about Voroshilov. The warrior of the ' Board of Merit ' had re-entered the army and already given a lecture to the officers of his regiment on 'Buddhism' or 'dynamism'—Pishchalkin did not quite remember which.

At the following station Litvinov had to wait a long time for the horses to be harnessed; it was very early morning, and he dropped asleep as he sat in his carriage. A voice that struck him as familiar woke him up; he opened his eyes....

Good heavens! Was it Mr. Gubaryov in a grey jacket and baggy bedroom trousers standing on the station steps and swearing?... No, it was not Gubaryov.... But what a remarkable likeness! Only this gentleman had a still broader and more predatory mouth, his lowering eyes had a still more ferocious look, his nose was bigger, his beard thicker, and his whole exterior heavier and more repulsive.

'Scou-oundrels, scou-oundrels!' he repeated slowly and malignantly, opening wide his wolfish mouth. 'Filthy peasants!... Here you have it ... your vaunted freedom ... one can't get any horses.... Scou-oundrels!'

'Scou-oundrels, scou-oundrels!' said another voice behind the door, and there appeared on the steps—also in a grey jacket and baggy bedroom trousers—this time undoubtedly the real Gubaryov himself, Stepan Nikolaevitch Gubaryov. 'Filthy peasants!' he went on in imitation of his brother (the other gentleman proved to be his elder brother, the 'bully' of the old school who managed his estate for him). 'They need a good thrashing, that's what I say; a punch on the snout, that's the freedom they need! The way they talk ... "the head of the *volost*"! I'd give it them!

But where is that M'sieur Roston? What is he
thinking about? It's the loafer's business to save us
trouble——'

'I've told you, brother, often enough, that he is
no use whatever,' the elder Gubaryov began, 'a
loafer is just what he is. It's only because of your
old ideas that you—— Moossieu Roston, Moossieu
Roston! Where the devil are you?'

'Roston! Roston!' the younger, the great
Gubaryov shouted. 'Call him properly, brother
Dorimedont Nikolaitch!'

'I'm calling him right enough, brother Stepan
Nikolaitch. Moossieu Roston!'

'Here I am, here I am!' a hurried voice was heard,
and from behind the corner of the cottage popped
out—Bambaev.

Litvinov fairly gasped. A shabby, braided jacket
with torn sleeves flapped dejectedly round the unfortunate enthusiast's body; his features had not
exactly changed, but somehow got drawn and twisted;
his anxious little eyes expressed servile fear and hungry
submissiveness; but a dyed moustache stuck out as
before above his puffy lips. The brothers Gubaryov
immediately began in concert to swear at him from the
top of the steps; he stood before them down in the
mud and humbly bending his back tried to soften
them by a timid little smile, crumpled his cap in his
red fingers, shuffled his feet, and muttered that the
horses would be brought at once.... But the brothers
went on abusing him until the younger happened to
glance at Litvinov. Whether it was that he recognized
him, or felt ashamed before a stranger, he suddenly

turned on his heels like a bear and biting his beard waddled into the station-house; the brother subsided instantly and, also turning round like a bear, walked after him. The great Gubaryov had evidently not lost his influence even in his native land.

Bambaev was about to follow the brothers. . . . Litvinov called him by name. He looked round, stared, and recognizing Litvinov rushed to him with open arms; but on reaching the carriage he took hold of the doors, rested his chest against them, and burst into a flood of tears.

'There, there, Bambaev!' Litvinov repeated, bending over him and touching him on the shoulder.

But he went on sobbing. 'You see—you see— what I've come to . . .' he muttered between his sobs.

'Bambaev!' the brothers thundered from within the cottage. Bambaev raised his head and hastily wiped his tears.

'How do you do, my dear?' he whispered. 'Good morning and good-bye! . . . You hear they're calling me.'

'But what wind brought you here?' Litvinov asked, 'and what does it all mean? I thought they were calling for a Frenchman——'

'I am their . . . house-manager, butler,' Bambaev answered, pointing his finger in the direction of the house. And they've made me into a Frenchman just for a joke. What will you have! I had nothing to live on, I've been done out of my last penny, so I was ready enough to put my head into the noose! I can't afford to be on my dignity.'

' Has *he* been long in Russia? And how did he part from his comrades? '

' Eh, brother, all that's done with.... You see, the wind has changed ... Madame Suhanchikov, Matryona Semyonovna, he simply kicked out. In her distress she went to Portugal.'

' How, to Portugal? What next ! '

' Yes, brother, to Portugal, with two Matryonovtsi.'

' With whom? '

' Matryonovtsi—that's how the members of her party are called.'

' So Matryona Semyonovna has a party? A large one? '

' Just those two people. And it will soon be six months since *he* returned here. Other people have been arrested, but nothing's been done to him. He's living in the country with his brother, and you should hear him now——'

' Bambaev ! '

' Coming, Stepan Nikolaitch, coming ! And you, my dear fellow, are flourishing? Enjoying life? Well, that's a good thing. Where are you off to now? ... It's been such a surprise.... Do you remember Baden? Ah, those were the days ! By the way, do you remember Bindasov? Would you believe it, he's dead. He got a job as an excise officer, had a fight in a pub, and they broke his head for him with a billiard cue. Yes, yes, we've fallen on hard times ! But still I'll say: Russia—what a country ! Look at that pair of geese, now: why, in the whole of Europe you'll find nothing like them ! Real Arzamas geese ! '

After paying this last tribute to his ineradicable craving for enthusiasm, Bambaev ran to the station cottage where his name was again being called, accompanied with vigorous expletives.

By the end of that day Litvinov was approaching Tatyana's estate. The small house where his former betrothed lived stood on a hill over a small river and was surrounded by a recently planted garden. The house too was quite new, only just built, and could be seen a long way off from the fields on the other side of the river. Litvinov saw it at a distance of nearly two miles, with its sharply outlined upper storey and a number of windows glowing vividly in the rays of the setting sun. He began to feel secretly anxious after leaving the last station, and now he was in a tumult of confusion: joyful confusion, but with a tinge of fear.... 'How will they meet me?' he thought. 'How shall I come before her?'

To distract himself he spoke to the driver, a dignified peasant with a grey beard, who had nevertheless charged him for twenty miles while the distance was less than seventeen. He asked the man whether he knew the Shestov ladies.

'The Shestovs? To be sure. They're kind ladies, there's no gainsaying. They doctor us, too, they do. Regular doctors! People go to them from all over the place. Yes, indeed, no end of people. If, let's say, any one is ill or cuts himself or anything, he goes to them straight away and they're sure to give him some lotion or powders or a plaster—and it's all right: it helps. And they won't accept any payment: we won't have it, they say, we're not doing it for money.

236

They've started a school, too ... but there's nothing in that!'

While the driver talked, Litvinov gazed intently at the house. A woman in white came out on to the balcony, stood there for a while, and disappeared. . . . 'Can it be she?' His heart gave a jump. 'Hurry up!' he called to the driver, who urged on the horses. A few more minutes and the carriage drove in at the open gates. Kapitolina Markovna was already standing on the steps, beside herself with excitement, clapping her hands, and calling out: 'I knew him, I was the first to know him! It's he! It's he! ... I knew!'

Litvinov jumped out of the carriage without giving time to the page-boy to open the carriage doors, and, hastily embracing Kapitolina Markovna, rushed into the house, across the hall into the parlour. . . . Overcome with confusion, Tatyana stood before him. She looked at him with her kind friendly eyes (she had grown thinner, but it suited her) and held out her hand to him. But he did not take her hand, he fell on his knees before her. She was utterly unprepared for this and did not know what to do, what to say. Tears came into her eyes. She was frightened, but her whole face lit up with joy—'Grigory Mihailitch, what are you doing?' she said—and he went on kissing the hem of her gown. He recalled with a melting heart how in Baden he had also knelt at her feet. . . . But then—and now!

'Tanya,' he kept repeating. 'Tanya! have you forgiven me, Tanya?'

'Aunt, aunt, what is he doing?' Tatyana turned to Kapitolina Markovna as she came into the room.

'Don't hinder him, don't hinder him, Tanya,' the good old lady answered. 'You see, he's come to surrender.'

It is time to end, however; and indeed there is nothing to add; the reader will guess for himself. . . . But what about Irina?

She is just as lovely in spite of being thirty; young men without number fall in love with her and would do so even more, if . . . if . . .

Reader, will you come with us for a few minutes to Petersburg, to one of the best houses there? Look: there is before you a large room furnished, we won't say luxuriously—that expression is too low—but with grave and imposing dignity. Do you feel a certain tremor of timid abasement? Know then: you have entered a temple, a temple consecrated to the highest propriety, benevolent virtue, in short, to things above. A secret, 'actually secret'[1] stillness enfolds' you. Velvet curtains over the doors, velvet curtains over the windows, a thick-pile carpet on the floor—all seem designed and adapted for subduing and softening all harsh sounds and strong sensations. Carefully shaded lamps inspire sedate and sober sentiments; a decorous odour pervades the stagnant air; even the samovar on the table hisses modestly and with restraint. The lady of the house, a person of importance in Petersburg society, speaks almost inaudibly; she always speaks as though there were somebody very ill, almost dying, in the room; other ladies, in imitation

[1] Untranslatable allusion to the rank of 'Actual secret councillor of state.' (Translator's note.)

of her, barely whisper; and her sister, who pours out the tea, moves her lips without any sound at all, so that a young man, who has accidentally come to the temple of decorum, is at a loss to understand what she wants of him, while she murmurs for the sixth time ' *Voulez-vous une tasse du thé ?* ' Dignified-looking young men can be seen in the corners; gentle obsequiousness shines in their eyes; their ingratiating expression is mild and serene; numerous orders of merit gleam softly on their breasts. The conversation, too, is gentle: it touches upon religious and patriotic subjects, F. N. Glinka's *Mystic Drop*, our mission in the East, the monasteries and brotherhoods in White Russia. From time to time liveried footmen move noiselessly across the soft carpet; their huge calves encased in tight, silk stockings shake soundlessly at every step; the respectful tremor of the hefty muscles only increases the general impression of decorum, benevolence, and reverence.... It's a temple ! It's a temple !

' Have you seen Madame Ratmirov to-day?' one great lady asks blandly.

' I met her to-day at Lise's,' the hostess answers like an Aeolian harp. ' I am sorry for her ... she has an embittered mind ... *elle n'a pas la foi.*'

' Yes, yes,' the great lady acquiesces. ' If I remember rightly it was Pyotr Ivanitch said of her—and said very truly—*qu'elle a* . . . *qu'elle a* . . . an embittered mind.'

' *Elle n'a pas la foi,*' the hostess's voice melts like the smoke of incense. ' *C'est une âme égarée.* She has an embittered mind.'

239

'She has an embittered mind,' her sister repeats with her lips only.

And that is why not all the young men fall in love with Irina. They are afraid of her . . . afraid of her 'embittered mind.' That is a stock phrase about her; like all phrases, it contains a grain of truth. And not only young men are afraid of her: so are grown-up people, men in high places, and even 'personages.' No one can detect more truly and subtly a petty or ridiculous trait in a person's character, no one else has the gift of branding it so pitilessly with an unforgettable word. . . . That word stings all the more because it comes from fragrant, beautiful lips. . . . It is hard to say what is happening in her heart; but in the crowd of her adorers not one is rumoured to be the man of her choice.

Irina's husband is moving fast along the path which the French call the path of distinctions. The stout general outruns him; the indulgent one remains behind. In the same town where Irina lives, lives also our friend Sozont Potugin; he does not see her often and there is no special need for her to keep up their connection. . . . The little girl who was entrusted to his care died not long ago.

This book, designed by
William B. Taylor
is a production of
Edito-Service S.A., Geneva

Printed in Switzerland

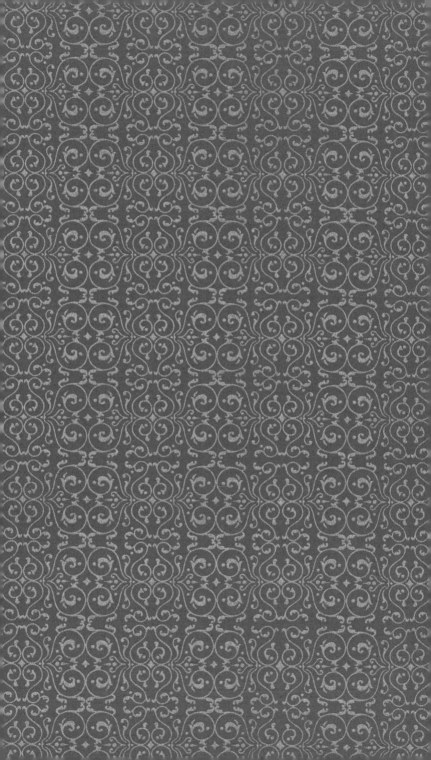